For My Pap.

Editors: Andreas Petrossiants, Michael Bottomley,

Dylan Brown, Cynthia Santiglia

Say Wow Publishing

BOOK CHAPTERS

Chapter 1

Immigration.

We all have a past, but some
remember it in vivid detail and carry it
with them like suitcases

The Roots

Fuckin' Roman. I still wonder what made me climb in the car with that crazy guy. When you are sitting there wondering "what the fuck am I doing here?" and "how do I get out of here?" Roman might just happen to you and twirl your life like a hurricane. Roman was the type of young Russian man that people conjure up in their heads when they think "oh, that Russian. He is probably doing something illegal," but still, they would be charmed by his words, shot at you like arrows to appeal to your inner gods and demons. As far as I could tell, I was not the typical young Russian man myself. And to be fair, Roman was far from the norm. Some people would say there is a magical magnetism that exists: like attracts like, opposite attracts opposite, drunk attracts drunk, or something like that. Whether I was Roman's brother from another immigrant mother or his complete opposite doesn't matter anymore because I believe the universe definitely had a hand in it.

My parents immigrated to the United States from Moscow in 1993, a few years after the famous political coup of '91. Though my mom and dad always loved Russia and stood at the front lines against the tanks, fighting for democracy, the corruption and mafia killed all opportunity to be honest in business. People were dying mysteriously, and everyone's life had a price. Everyone was an entrepreneur dabbling in anything they could get their hands on. My father was trying to work as the middleman connecting buyers with sellers. When there was not much to eat and selection at the stores was slim, sugar suddenly became a high commodity. During one of my father's biggest transactions, the mafia brought him a suitcase full of American dollars in exchange for 50 trucks loaded with sugar. When the sugar supplier suddenly disappeared and the mafia told him they were going to come after his family, the plan to immigrate to America materialized rather quickly. My parents were honest intellectual people who loved their family life and their vibrant friends. Almost everyone graduated from college and had proper education, but everyone lived paycheck-to-paycheck making just enough to get by since it was impossible to earn more the honest way.

Imported clothes for women were a luxury item. When there was news of the imported goods, such as women's dresses or shoes, there was talk about it for weeks. Women would try to buy the imported clothes and shoes from each other for higher prices, even though the sizes were all different most of the time.

Bananas! I loved bananas. My father would bring home bananas, a box full of them, and he would hide them from me and me little sister in the mezzanine. They were all green, but the knowledge that there were bananas ripening made it a holiday for as long as we had them.

That was the life, and in the midst of all that, there was our family and friends. My parents would host those parties—gatherings, really—and the house would be filled with their friends, music, laughter, drinking and great young energy. What special times those were! Two of my father's friends played guitars. Alec was the name of one of his friends, and the other one was called Ilusha. They were married to girlfriends and they would always try to outdo each other seeing who could perform a better song on an acoustic guitar to get the most crowd participation. Since most of the lyrics were improvised anyways those songs were the epic highlights of the evenings. They were such nice people, young, energetic, ambitious, and full of life trying to live and swim in the communist bullshit agenda that was all around them, yet they were still trying to have their young fun at the end of the seventies and early eighties. Each family had two kids each as if by some government limit, no more no less, one boy and one girl. In 1980's Moscow, this was the way of life. This is what made living exciting, looking forward to the next family or friend's gathering at our parents' house. What I took away from these party nights, and from my family in general, was simply that your family and friends are more important money.

So when my parents announced to my sister and me that we were moving to America, they didn't need to tell us too much. We understood, but at the same time, we were sad. Russia was our home. The only real idea I had about America came from the movies. I thought, it really was like in the movies. Hip-hop was becoming popular in Russia and when my friends and I heard the first few imported tapes of American rap such as Dr. Alban and MC Hammer we were in awe at their sneakers and the way

8

they danced. Of course, in the tender pre-puberty years, I wanted it all to be true. I was very excited for the move. I was going to be an American. I was going to live the Hollywoodized sparkle of the immigrant's American dream to a hip-hop soundtrack. I was going to be huge. Different. The only one. I thought, upon coming to States, that I was surely going to meet Rambo, and might run into the Terminator walking down the street.

Imagine my shock when I found out that I was one of 100's of not even just Russians, but more specifically Bukharian students at my high school in Forest Hills, Queens, and that my English was quite possibly the worst among all of them. Bukhara was one of the areas in the Asian region of Russia. In Russia, Bukharians were usually working at the bazaars or as taxicab drivers. Also, I was one of 5 Dmitrys'. I was happy that we landed in Queens since it was a melting pot of immigrants from different countries moving to the USA. Brooklyn was worse. It was the mecca of the Russian immigration since the 80's and completely didn't fit in with my plans of being an American.

I also quickly understood that hip-hop wasn't as hip among the Russian people here as it was in Russia. In the 90's a lot of black people listened to hip-hop. They were wearing jeans that hung low and constantly had to be pulled up , and they spray-painted subway cars. I didn't like their jeans style and I couldn't assimilate with them or even find any similarities at the time. Also they spoke strange English and swallowed their words making it undecipherable to me. They would come up with their own words. I had to listen hard and ask them to repeat what they said to understand. Bukharian immigrants I knew listened to techno and dance house music to impress girls. I hated that music; there was no soul in it just electronic beats and stupid lyrics. That's when I began discovering rock music and started sinking into Led Zeppelin, Pink Floyd and eventually someone recommended I listen to the Doors. As long as it had guitars I was into it, but the Doors in particular blew my mind with their lyrics, artistic approach to music writing and Jim Morrisson's medieval poet role he played on stage.

To separate myself from the pack of Russian immigrants, I changed my name to *Danny*. I thought that English name sounded better than the Russian one. Danny was simple, it had the same first letter as my Russian name and it sounded American. Also, some kids I knew at school changed their names, for example, this Bukharin guy, Viacheslav changed his name to Sam. Even Chinese immigrants were doing it, Xuang Lao was now John. Sure it was a bit confusing to have a guy named Danny have a thick Russian accent while ordering a cheeseburger, but you should have heard John say "Double Cheese Burger with Fries and Coke." I remember when I was working my first job at a bagel shop. Truck drivers with baseball hats and overalls would yell out their orders, "Two eggs on a roll with bacon and cheese," and I would give them a loaf of bread. They would get pissed. Yep. Danny sucked at English.

After two years of school my English still sucked, and the name *Danny* just sounded silly. I spoke Russian, my friends were Russian—I was Russian and at 16 it hit me that *Dmitry* is the name my mother gave me so I changed it back. There were American kids at school called "Xavier" and "Ronald." Those poor bastards, what kinds of names were those, anyways?

In schools in Russia, you learned things. Actually applicable things to use in everyday life: languages, math, or environment skills, such as how to put out a fire in the middle of the forest. In American schools, the things you learn, though also applicable in life, were entirely different. What I learned in school was that the *popularity contest* is real, and it's forever.

I knew I needed something to get me ahead, but after two years of forcing things to make me more American, I decided I needed to be myself. And I thought: music. I had started playing guitar back in Russia, and I loved the emotion I could put into it, but I wasn't very good at it.

Music was always there for me. A mysterious art that girls loved and guys wore like a cool leather jacket after they learned a few songs on the acoustic guitar. I realized what I didn't like, the techno music, country and rap. I knew that rock and roll was cool, and that Americans loved cool, and that I wanted Americans to love me.

Unfortunately for me, there was no rock band in school that I could join to learn an instrument. But there was a jazz band, and it needed a bass player. I didn't know the first thing about the bass, but I did know that I cared way more about making some American friends than I did about looking like an asshole.

If you know anything about jazz, you know that the bass is important. I can say with certainty that my bass playing was bad – so I walked myself away from the agony of being in a jazz band and learning note music. I was an awful player, but I liked how holding a guitar made me feel. This jazz band was far more than just a place where I got a new skill. It was a place where I made friends. American friends. Not all of them were American, but at least some of them were born here. What we couldn't communicate through English or Russian we communicated through music. That was our language. And it worked. Some guys would be sitting outside of the school showing off to each other a new song they learned by Jimi Hendrix on acoustic guitar while others listened and bummed cigarettes from each other. That was my world. I could associate with this desire to show off a new song, as opposed to my peers, who were riding around in shiny new cars with windows down blasting stupid techno with stupid words that didn't mean shit.

Meanwhile, my parents' parties continued in the United States. While parties in Russia carried a feeling of abyss because of the future's shitty unpredictability, America's parties were somber because of its predictability. Because most of my parents' friends were immigrants with children the same age as my sister and I, college was the question on everyone's mind. How should we pay for it? What should they study? The choice rested heavily on the parents. We had to carry forward the big *Immigrants in the Land of Opportunities* slogan.

Though I wanted to continue studying music, arts, and literature, my father insisted I look to the future and study computer science. I hated it. I knew that no matter how much I hated it, he would win. I obeyed my father. He scared me since childhood. His hand was heavy when he was frustrated and his frustrations didn't end at work. I made up for the other half with my grades in school. I remember in Russia when he came back from work, tired and frustrated and had to attend teacher – parent meetings at my school, afterwards my mom would run ahead of my father and yell "Dima hide!" there was nowhere to run, my room was small and there was only a balcony attached to it. (Dima – a short way of saying Dmitry in Russia.) I knew what came next was a proper belting. She would hold my father back for as long as she could. I was scared shitless and emotionally ruined after those teacher - parent meetings, although I have to say that teaching through the belt worked every time – for awhile. The following few weeks I had perfect grades, which motivated me only for a short time, and then grades would start sliding and there was another teacher – parent meeting and the same thing would happen all over again.

We were at the kitchen table having a fight about what my college career should be. I said that I didn't give a shit about computers. It's a fad, life has been going on for thousands of years without them, and it will go on without them just fine. I yelled, "Computers?! They're pointless!"

His eyes looked mad and hurt. They didn't cry, but you know when your father is hurting. He moved here for his daughter, his son and his wife. He was doing what was best for me and he told me that, but I was an 18 year old, and therefore a rebel without a real cause. In some way, I owed him something: the move to America, education, and the opportunities. I gave in. I said, "Fine. I'll do it." I thought about it for a moment, I stood up and added in conclusion, "But once that diploma is in my hand, I'm doing whatever I want with my life." He agreed.

For the first year I went to a city college in New York and then I transferred to a state university in Long Island to major in Information Systems. The very first teacher of my first computer class jumped on the podium, looked at everyone like a madman and said, "Look around you, you won't find half of your friends by the end of the semester, because I am going to make this class so hard you will quit, since computers are not a joke. They are for dedicated and serious people only." I thought, great, I am fucked, and he was right.

The workload was really intense, especially that first year and it was hard to have a campus life and to get properly drunk since some computer lab assignment was always due the next morning, but Russians always found a way to get drunk. We would get drunk early in the day and then go to a computer lab for the whole night until the last man standing. We would fall asleep on computer keyboards just to wake up and go back to classes. I seriously thought the whole time that this was nightmare and I was going to fail. During the first year finals, we were studying the whole night for the most important final exam and when the morning came I closed my eyes for a short nap. Turns out I was about to sleep through the most decisive exam and all of a sudden at 8:55AM my phone rang. I jumped up and answered the phone. There was no one on the line. I remembered I had an exam to take so I ran and was the last person admitted before they shut the doors. Surprisingly I passed with a C-, the lowest score ever, but a passing score nevertheless. I asked everyone I knew if someone called me at 8:55am, but no one knew anything. Probably God called me, who knows. I graduated university with a surprisingly decent GPA. Being faithful to my rebellion I finished my school studies in 3.5 years and I felt now I could do whatever I wanted. I had kept my word.

When I finally got my diploma I threw it on the table in front of my father and said to him, "Now I am going to do what I want." He was proud and said, "Go ahead, but still think about your future." Little did I know what I studied would always put food on the table even when things were rough and I was down on my luck.

I never became fully Americanized, nor was I completely Russian. I was a weird mix. I fit in with Russians immediately since we spoke the same language and had similar upbringing, but I was too American for them since I preferred to speak English and I lacked nostalgic notions for the motherland. I was also proud to know all the latest American rock bands. I liked having American friends and speaking slang, but for them I was still a weird Russian who tried to speak English. I was always stuck in the middle somewhere, holding my ground of uniqueness and not striving to become one or the other. Although that didn't prove to be easy when choosing friends; they wanted that assuredness that you were just like them, but that's something I never offered anyone. Not even my own reflection in the mirror.

Chapter 2

Vlad

His glance resembled wilderness
and some magic spells at work

Meeting Vlad

I was twenty-two years old. I had graduated from the university a year before, and already held a full-time job at a prestigious company. I really wanted to go abroad and live in London, but this job materialized rather unexpectedly. The pay was through the roof. I was stunned at such a prospect, but hey, it was the Dotcom boom. We all joked about it back then: if you skateboarded and knew Photoshop you got immediately offered 60 grand a year. I decided to take the job. The pay was great, but it ended shortly after 9/11 happened. One day I came to work and the Twin Towers were destroyed. I was standing in the office in Jersey City looking across the river, where the Twin Towers used to be, the smoke still rising, and thinking to myself, I could have been under that rubble. I was a lucky son of a bitch. I would have been under that wreck, had I not stayed at my friend Vinni's house. Music saved me. We had rehearsed the night before. Of course, we had one drink too many and I slept through the early bus into the city, so I took a later bus. From the windows of that bus, I saw the 2nd plane hitting the 2nd tower. It was hell. People yelled on the bus, some of them cried, some of them just yelled out of fear of the unknown. I couldn't say anything, I was just silent. Everything went to shit after that. Priorities shifted rather quickly for everyone.

After the job was over, I was still living with my parents in Kew Gardens, Queens and I needed to move out badly. My dad wasn't happy that my decisions so far had consisted of what brand of booze I would get a hangover with, when's my next rehearsal, and where is the next party. He urged me to think about my future. I couldn't stand anymore living with constant disapproval of me not looking for another job. Work wasn't an interesting prospect to me. I really was just trying to start a band while they were really hoping my guitar playing was just a hobby. On top of it all, they didn't approve of me dating a woman 9 years older than me, since she was detonating all kinds of anti-parents propaganda with her extravagant lifestyle, starting with being a concubine to their 22-year-old son. They thought she was evil and responsible for all kinds of mayhem going on in my head. They were probably right. What sucked was that I was broke and I had nothing saved. My ex and I, we specialized in spending my paycheck in one weekend on drinks, blow, parties and eating out at the finest restaurants of New York City.

I still lived in Kew Gardens. I grew up there and had some wonderful memories, but I learned to despise it as well. It was an old and quiet Jewish neighborhood right by the Long Island Railroad train station that took you into Manhattan in 15 minutes. There was only one attractive street block with European looking stores and houses on Lefferts Boulevard. We had one bum whose name was Paris, who used to own a porno cinema and then sold it. Somehow I thought, if you sold something you would be making money and not be a bum, but in his case it wasn't so. What did I care? Paris was our friend: the friend of the youth. Everyone knew him so we gave him money, drinks and smoked cigarettes together. There was one great pizzeria, called Denny's. Also there was one more cool historical fact, that Charlie Chaplin lived a few streets down from the train station back at the turn of the century in one of those old brick private houses. No one exactly knew which house, but the thought of it was comforting. For the most part, it was a sleepy town where not much was going on, aside from a handful of young Russian immigrants who were trying to live, party and get high while making sense of what they should be doing with their lives in New York.

One of those immigrants, from Ukraine (part of the former Soviet Union), was Vlad. He moved to New York from Kharkov, Ukraine at the age of 21. He was 25 now, good natured, a network engineer with an intense temperament, love for writing poetry, medieval sword fighting, bard music and a knack for getting into all kinds of weird troubles. If you looked up his last name on the family tree, it traced back all the way to Rurik dynasty around 1000AD. Viking prince Rurik was the founding father of Kiev Rus, which later spawned Russia. So as you can imagine - I didn't have a simple friend.

When I met him the first time, he was crossing the street wearing a long black cape, dirty boots and a long wooden stick. I didn't know what to think. I was seventeen and never ran into such weird characters. His glance resembled wilderness and some magic spells at work. He looked as if he walked out of some Lord of the Rings book and straight onto sleepy streets of our old Jewish neighborhood in Kew Gardens.

One day this old computer at my parent's house had some network problems. I called my friend Vlad to help me out. My parents asked me if I was sure that I wanted to ask Vlad, since he had a reputation for, let's say it lightly, not having the best luck. I assured them it would be fine.

Vlad responded to my call happily and came rather quickly. He quickly took apart the whole computer although I was not sure why he had to take it apart to fix some network problems. Nevertheless, after about an hour of trying to fix it, Vlad proclaimed that he couldn't fix our computer issue without his tools so he went home to pick them up. We waited for a while, but that night Vlad didn't come back, nor the following night or 2 weeks after that. Wondering where Vlad went, I asked around and found out that Vlad went home that day and found his old friend, Shurik waiting for him with few bottles of something strong. Shurik was a rather simple guy and a good friend of Vlad. I think they knew each other back in Ukraine. I never really knew much about Shurik except that he was a nice guy, he had an easy going personality and when he got drunk and high he started speaking as if he was meowing. Naturally, Vlad and Shurik finished those bottles.

Vlad loved sword fighting and fencing, so he had some fencing foils lying around the house. Every time his friends would come over to have few rounds of drinks and smoke a few joints he would try to get his friends to fence with him. Not everyone agreed. Vlad challenged his friend to a fencing match. During that drunken fencing match Shurik accidentally poked Vlad through his eye nerve, which led to Vlad partially losing vision in one eye. I don't know what's more retarded, Vlad challenging his opponent to a drunken fencing match or Shurik for actually agreeing to such a crazy idea. That story should have warned me not to move in with Vlad, but we don't really make good decisions until we make a whole bunch of bad ones first. I decided moving in with Vlad would be the best way to get out of my parents house and to start feeling like an independent adult.

Vlad's apartment was in a town-house complex right next to a cemetery in Kew Gardens, Queens. Even though it was a small studio, we were both unemployed and splitting rent was way more appealing to both of us financially. Plus, it was few streets down from where my parents lived, so I could always stop by for a satisfying meal if need be. It was all decided, and I moved into Vlad's studio apartment.

The (Im)Perfect Lifestyle

Vlad was a very social guy and had a lot of friends. On any random night you could expect people just showing up at the apartment unannounced, and Vlad never turned away friends without a proper drink, a cigarette and a long conversation. Living with Vlad had a very similar vibe to life on college campus.

At Vlad's apartment there were always people playing acoustic guitars, discussing relationships, crying, laughing, drinking, watching movies and smoking joints. The apartment complex consisted of two-floor townhouses standing in the circle with a very nice and lush garden in the middle. All the entrances to apartments were from the garden side so you could pretty much do whatever you wanted and cops would never ever see you. Sometimes when the little studio got too cramped and we couldn't breathe the cigarette smoke anymore, we would go outside to the garden in the front of the apartment, lay down in the grass, smoke a joint and look up at the stars. It was a perfectly healthy lifestyle for a twenty-two year old that didn't have responsibilities or any direction.

When it became light outside everyone would fall asleep in the middle of their phrases still holding on to their cigarettes, cd's still playing and unfinished conversations still hanging in the air. Next morning, they would wake up, light up their cigarettes, cook up some wild concoctions for breakfast, get more beers, get drunk again, finish those beers, sober up and finally when the drinks were finished they would go home. Very often a handful of people would remain and if Vlad couldn't challenge anyone anymore to a fencing match then he would challenge them to a game of chess. Before the game, everyone would take long puffs on a joint and then sit behind the chessboard for hours, too stoned to think. Vlad won most of the time, but sometimes Vlad would get even more stoned. Then the others would accidentally win. After a few games of chess people would finally leave, but in few hours new people would arrive and things would continue in the same fashion.

The fridge was as fascinating as a flying saucer. Often we would stare inside it, but wouldn't see anything. To fight our fierce hangovers we tried some bizarre recipes such as: cold cereal with water, Chinese rice with jam or sardines and watermelon. Don't try this at home! It tasted nasty!

Vlad and I were the only actual residents of the small studio apartment, but my best friend Vinni was also riding on the unemployed debauchery experience we specialized in. He would stay with us for days and sleep in the corner on the floor, covered by a throw and a pillow. Partly because he was working in the city and it was easier for him to get to work from Queens rather than from bumble fuck New Jersey, and also Vinni was like a brother to me from another immigrant mother.

We met during my freshman year in Baruch College. We were both standing outside chewing on a cigarette butt each discussing some trivial bullshit with our private circle of friends. I had an edgy raver look back then. I wore wide legged pants, some red t-shirt, military black backpack and a blue baseball hat. The only association with the mother ship was a small Russian flag I sewed onto my backpack. Vinni, having guessed but still being unsure of my origins, asked where was I from in a thick Russian accent. I answered with a smirk, making a very good guess where he was from by his thick accent, "Same country as you are." We laughed, and after I found out that he lived in Kew Gardens, in a building across from mine, had calluses on his finger tips from playing a lot of guitar just like me and he listened to the same bands, that sealed our friendship. Our tight drinking bond was inseparable so we formed a band together called Table Dreams. We needed a bassist so I said, "Fuck it I will be a bass player although I was a guitar player." I actually got pretty good at bass, but secretly I always wanted to play guitar. Nevertheless, we were crafting our own style of music called Metal-Disco-Punk, and when Vlad wasn't around we were practicing at Vlad's apartment. We specialized in writing danceable grooves that turned into metal progressions and punchy riffs with song names like "Immigrants Song" and "Mom it's Time to Move Out." We earned the respect and a bit of fame in close immigrant circles. Some people seeing a demand for immigrant rock music opened Russian Rock Club and started organizing concerts in Manhattan and our band Table Dreams was invited many times to play at CBGB, L'amours and other legendary spots. The only thing was that Vinni and I, being the immigrant punks as we were, hated the whole Russian Rock Club idea since we thought, "why would you open a Russian Rock Club living in New York, a capital of the world?" So we sang in English as a middle finger to the whole idea. They still loved it and we put on high-energy memorable vodka fueled shows. During one show, I dressed up as Mozart with a classy white wig and we opened the show with Grieg's classical piece "Peer Gynt Suite No.1" We started it very slow and converted it to speed metal in a matter of seconds. We also brought a black percussionist with a train whistle, and we played all 4 songs that we had at that time. We managed to deliver the most memorable performance of our life. Unfortunately, I didn't remember anything from that night, since I was so drunk I completely blacked out during the performance. I guess I went to some performer's heaven and back, but nevertheless those were our Table Dreams times, and they were fun. Hence Vinni and I formed our little Table Dreams headquarters at Vlad's studio apartment.

Beside Vlad, Vinni and I, my grandmother's cocker spaniel would also join our motley crew, and things went really out of whack. The story was that my grandmother really wanted a dog in America, so she bought a cute puppy with long ears and orange fur and gave him a real American name - "Tommy." Instead of training him she was feeding him kielbasa under the table, which spoiled him from the beginning. Without a proper training routine, Tommy grew up into the most capricious, manner-less, self-entitled, vain and psychotic dog you could ever raise. He was already seven years old, but he was still pissing on her carpets and raping her pillows. After a while my grandma couldn't handle his abusive relationship with her furniture, and she was asking me what to do. Vlad had a soft spot for cocker spaniels since he owned one when he was a kid. After seeing Tommy, Vlad volunteered to adopt him for few months and see how things go. He didn't suspect that Tommy was a crazy son of a bitch. My grandmother was very happy with that arrangement for about a few months and then she started missing the little bastard, "Where is my little Tommy? My little cute spaniel, I forgive him everything!"

Meanwhile, Tommy would shit, piss, rape, tear and bark at everyone who walked through our front door. When you pet Tommy, he would start growling and any wrong move led to his jaws snapping.

Vlad tried to educate Tommy how a proper dog should behave. It looked something like this: Vlad would stand there and look down at Tommy, then point with his finger at the new puddle Tommy left in the middle of the house. Tommy would growl back at Vlad, ready for anything. Vlad would try to give Tommy his hand to sniff, so the dog knows who the man of the house is and who should obey whom. That would have worked with any other normal dog, but with Tommy never. Tommy thought that he was the owner of the house, so he would bite Vlad's hand. It happened every other day. Tommy and Vlad were very stubborn.

Vlad never carried keys to his own apartment so everyone that knew Vlad would simply climb through the window. One time, Vlad, Tommy and I weren't at the apartment and only Vinni was staying over. Vinni apparently didn't know about the window entrance trick. All of a sudden, he wakes up and sees this guy trying to climb through the window. His facial expression was silently screaming, "What the hell? Thief?" Meanwhile, this guy was a good friend of Vlad's. His name was Andrei, and he had just gotten married to Alisa, a fiery bohemian Russian blonde woman with a deep love for poetry and drama.

If Dostoevsky met her, she would have been the main character of one of his books, and he would have spent pages describing her because she had that powerful presence of untamed beauty, hurt pride, deep existential conflict and classic Russian debauchery. When she was sober she was deep, charming and reflective, but when she drank her charm turned into a street thug attitude and men were something to despise and to cry on at the same time. She was a total mess. Andrei was a hippie with long curly hair who was hopelessly in love with her and tried all he could to appease her. According to her, he was no angel, and she always found ways to reproach him for the wrong way he treated her at some bar, or on the phone, or a year before.

You could understand Vinni's predicament as he was eyeing heavy objects in the room to protect the apartment from this thief. Vinni didn't know that Andrei had spoken with Vlad on the phone earlier or that Vlad told them to spend their wedding night in his apartment. Andrei, having sensed that Vinni would suspect him to be a hairy thief, had to say something smart so he said, "Stay calm! I am one of us!"

Vinni thought hard and asked, "Who is us?"

Andrei replies, "You know, us! One of Vlad's friends. I got married today."

Vinni slowly realized that Vlad probably forgot to tell him, so Vinni mumbled something and let him in. Meanwhile Andrei's bride, Alisa, couldn't really walk into the house; she was completely disabled by alcohol and love and had to be carried inside. Andrei understood that he should put his new wife to sleep in her disheveled condition, but he was just as drunk as she was. He asked half-sleeping Vinni to help him carry his new wife to bed by grabbing her legs. Vinni was too sleepy to protest so he shrugged his shoulders and proceeded to move her onto the bed. As they stood her up Andrei was holding her by the armpits, he asked Vinni to politely take off her pants since it was hot in the room. Vinni grumbled at this request, but Andrei was too busy holding her from falling. As Vinni was pulling off her pants Alisa's hippie unshaven bush was staring Vinni directly in the face. Andrei smiled, shrugged his shoulders and said, "Excuse us." Vinni made a long face and tried hard pretending not to notice anything unusual and they just threw her on the bed to sleep. Alisa simply snorted at that motion, turned towards the wall and fell asleep soundly.

Next morning Alisa woke up yelling, "*Gde moi trusi svolochi? Kto s menya snyal moi trusi vchera?*" (Where are my underwear you bastards? Who took off my underwear yesterday?) Of course she didn't remember she didn't have them in the first place, but she was still wondering whether it was her husband or Vinni who got a glimpse of her privates. She was pretty pissed. When Vinni was telling me this story I was laughing so hard. Those situations happened a lot since no one actually owned keys to Vlad's apartment aside from me.

Vlad's mother would sometimes come over and would start accusing him of not working and leading a questionable lifestyle. In the mind of every immigrant parent was this justification. Because they had to go through such struggles to bring their children to America, their children owed them for the rest of their life and they shouldn't spend their time on arts, contemplating life, drinking and not working in the land of opportunities. They would say, "Vlad stop this nonsense lifestyle and get a job!" He would reply, "Ma, don't tell me what to do! I am looking for a job, my last one sucked, because…" and he would give a long explanation of why he didn't like his last job. After that his mother would leave and come back in a week or two with the same question.

As far as being roommates, we were pretty dysfunctional. Never mind the fact that the apartment consisted of one living room, a small kitchen, bathroom and a small closet. The apartment was always a fucking mess. Every time a question of cleaning came about Vlad loved to debate about it. I was younger and less experienced at such verbal diarrheas, especially in Russian, so most of the time I was pissed that somehow our debates ended up with Vlad having the upper hand. Of course he had a valid closing statement that it was his apartment first and I was just paying rent, but the bastard always made sure to stress that fact which annoyed the hell out of me. He finalized our discussions by throwing a few jabs below the belt with jokes mostly of a belittling homosexual nature. I would leave the apartment for few hours to calm down my anger.

I think at the core of it all, Vlad clearly had a Napoleon complex. I was way taller than him, and he was uncomfortable. That's why he was constantly trying to prove his superiority, if not by height then at least by reason. He laughed at me, and I didn't waste time making fun of him among my friends. Although, deep down I knew he was a good friend, and I was thankful he let me live with him in a tiny studio. I was ready to do anything to get away from living with my parents and their righteous ways. Still he drove me nuts every other day.

K.S.P

Every summer Russian immigrants living in New York organized this camping/music festival in the woods called K.S.P. (Klub Samodelnoi Pesni - translated from Russian - *Club of Bard Song*.)
K.S.P. is a 3-day festival, inspired and attended by Russian immigrants who love singing bard songs around the campfire to get down with their roots. At K.S.P. everyone camped out and there was no stage. All acoustic performances were around the fire pits. It had a very loose vibe to it. It resembled an idea for Woodstock festival, lets get together in one place for the sake of music. However, if the slogan of the hippies of the sixties was Peace, Music and Love, K.S.P.'s slogan could have been: Music, Camping, Sex, Drugs and Vodka. I attended this festival for few years in a row, and it was definitely a place to let go and kick back.

There was this noticeable division between the older and younger generations. While the older immigrants would be sitting around the fire singing intellectual bard songs to each other and getting nostalgic about the way things were in the Soviet Union, the herd of youth that Russian immigrants raised would have no problems with the way things currently are. It was a perfect anything goes type of place where, for 3 days in a row, you could consume insane amounts of vodka, smoke marijuana, eat psychedelic mushrooms, ecstasy and whatever else you could get your hands on, as long as it was within the confines of the campground. At night, the camping tents would be shaking from the law of intoxicated attraction working on the very basic level, and therefore many babies were conceived at K.S.P. Many boyfriends found themselves with different girlfriends in the morning, and many girlfriends found themselves with different husbands. Being a Russian meant that you would always blame vodka for everything you did the night before and you would vow to give up drinking forever. Well, at least until the next weekend.

The summer of 2002 I decided not to go, but my roommate Vlad couldn't miss another golden opportunity to let his freak flag fly at K.S.P. so he went as usual. I told him I stayed home because I had to rehearse with my band, but really I wanted a rest from Vlad and everything that came along with him. The whole weekend I was enjoying the intense peace and quiet in the house that I missed so much. Finally, around Sunday evening, Vlad arrived with some guests. The minute he walked in he started yelling out my name, "Dimka, Dimka!" That's what he called me: a kind of a belittling way of saying Dmitry. I didn't mind it. He continued speaking fast, "KSP was very *klassno* (super cool), too bad you couldn't go. I met some cool people they are going to stay over for few nights." Even though there wasn't enough silence for a few days, I was still glad to see him all happy. It sucked having Vlad as a roommate, but he was still my weird friend.

Chapter 3

The Meeting

Do you want to know why elephants don't fly?

Let me tell you after I take this shot

Unexpected Guests

I recognized one of the guests; it was Shurik. I shook his hand and moved on to the next guest. He introduced himself as Roman. His handshake was strong and firm. I liked it when people gave me a strong handshake; to me it always signified a strong character. He was broad shouldered, sported a little musketeer mustache, a tanned face and small dark eyes. I thought to myself, what a Russian name. Electricians or carpenters were usually named Roman in my neighborhood in Moscow, and they were all alcoholics. I chuckled quietly and then, looking at him, I continued to myself, what a funny looking dude. He was wearing a navy parachute hat, shorts, orange t-shirt, and flip-flops. His face had crow lines around his eyes, an imprint of someone who laughed a lot in his life. It was one of those moments when you know that something is about to unfold, but you don't know exactly what it is yet. He gave off the impression of someone that had lived and traveled a lot.

Roman introduced his girlfriend. "Carla," she said. She was a nice American girl, soft-spoken, rather simple in facial features; although her shaved head gave her an unusual and a very artistic look. They looked like a really odd couple, but their oddness made it work. Roman had a certain brutal honesty about him, which he expressed through sarcastic jabs that he threw mostly at Vlad. Vlad retorted them with ease. It seemed that Roman was enjoying being himself immensely. In 5 minutes after he walked in, he was already singing some Bard song to Shurik, claiming that he forgot to sing this one back at K.S.P.

That same night the party started. Other friends of Vlad's came over that didn't attend K.S.P. but wanted to hear all about it. We went to the store, got some beers, rolled up new joints, and our little studio apartment was alive again. Nothing had changed, although this time something was different. It almost seemed as if things were way looser, people were way drunker, songs were louder – and at the head of all this was Roman. It seemed as if he never went overboard even though he drank as much as everyone. He was, somehow, always in control of his actions. He would wink at Carla and me and say, "Dimka, let's go to the store. We ran out of beer." I would say, "Sure, let's go." Roman seemed very confident in who he was at that moment and his confidence was inspiring. He intrigued me, since everything seemed easy for him.

He was winking infectiously at everyone saying, "Davai, Davai" (Come on, come on) to help him sing and join in his good times. He always knew what to say and do to make sure people had a good time. Whether you wanted booze, a joint, or a good song. He had it. His silent motto was, you are either with me or you are against me. I joined him, as I was no sucker when it came to partying. He reminded me of my father.

My father was a heavyweight champion when it came to drinking and good times. At every party, my dad would automatically become the

L.O.T.P. (Life of the Party). He would have enough time to joke, take shots, shower all the ladies with compliments, starting with my mom, then dance with them all until they dropped. My dad was as graceful as a ballet dancer, even though he had a big belly. Everyone loved him, men and women, because he had that big presence and a gift for entertaining people that no one else had. There was not a party, a wedding or an anniversary that my parents attended where people didn't remember my father. For that one moment, he made their lives mean something, and let them forget where they came from. I on the other hand was somewhat different from my dad.

I was an artist and a musician. When I was offstage I was kind of a seeker and an observer, a sponge that would watch and soak in the world around me. When I would take the stage: that was my time to shine. Something changed inside, and I was transformed into a performer. Everything that I saw in real life around me I acted out, mimicked and performed on stage.

For Roman, life was his stage. When he called out to everyone to start doing shots without using their hands, everyone followed along. When he asked people to start doing cart wheels after taking a pull on a joint everyone did it, just to feel that extra high that he claimed would happen afterwards. It seemed as if he specialized in pushing the limits. He reminded me of my dad a lot. My dad was also known for getting everyone drunk. People would usually come up with reasons for not drinking due to having to get up early the next day, or they had to drive, and my dad would say, "Do you want to know why elephants don't fly? Let me tell you after this shot." Seven shots later they didn't have to go anywhere and everyone was merry and happy. Roman added an extra element of danger and realness to everything he did.

I was having a blast hanging out with Roman. I thought this guy was different for a few reasons. Although he was born in Russia, he spent a good number of years in Los Angeles. You could feel that about him. The way he spoke English without an accent, unlike immigrants from New York, and the way he dressed was very American. He knew all the lyrics to songs by such rap artists as Notorious BIG, Jay-Z and Dr. Dre that only an American teen would know by heart. At the same time, he was a mountain climber in Russia who loved bard songs – a paradox of some sort. I liked him because he didn't have any concept of needing to be somewhere else. He was 100% present here and now.

I also noticed he was damn good at crossing that invisible line of moral code. That thin line that exists in every normal person's mind and separates the things into two categories: those that are ok to do and those that are not. He was constantly testing how far he could take it with you, either with his words or his actions. It was a fun game to him. I was just watching his games and I wasn't sure if I liked it or not. He was sort of the Russian version of Neal Cassady, the friend who inspired Jack Kerouac. In few days, I totally bonded with Roman. To some degree, I was also jealous of his source of freedom: he owned it and was connected to it. I wanted to be like him. I wanted to know what made him not give a fuck about what people thought and just go with his own flow.

Chapter 4

The Brighton Beach Escapade

We got from Queens to
Brooklyn in 7 minutes

The Hangover

Slowly, Vlad started realizing that Roman and his girlfriend Carla were not looking for another place to stay and that they didn't want to leave, either. Roman and Carla seemed very content staying with us. We had been drinking excessively for a week without taking a break. I was getting bored with this drinking routine. Vinni and I didn't practice for a week. We didn't have a drummer again so we didn't have any shows scheduled in the near future. Hangovers became fiercer, and Vlad became more annoying.

This particular morning, Vlad had a serious hangover and he became very irritated with his guests. Vlad took me aside and started mumbling, "Dimka, it's time we told them to go, because I am getting kind of sick of this Roman guy. All he wants to do is party."

I replied to him, "Hey, you brought him here, you tell him," I wasn't going to tell Roman that he had to go, since I didn't want to be that guy. Judging by Roman's responses to people's work schedules he didn't like any mention of reality or constraints on his freedom.

Since I had to survive somehow, I would take on small projects on the side doing some web design work for a friend. He would pay me a little bit and that was enough to get by and pay rent with. I set up my office in a closet since it was the only space to get away from Vlad and have some sort of a silence. I would have put my bed there too, if there was room. I did agree hangovers got in the way of my work. As I was pondering what Vlad said, Roman interrupted me and said, "Dimon, let's go to Brighton Beach in Brooklyn and take a swim – it's getting hot." I thought, Brighton Beach?

Brighton Beach was everything I despised about being Russian. It was a mecca of Russian immigrants who still dressed as if they lived in the 80's. The minute you tell someone in USA that you are Russian, you get put into a box of stereotypes and the first one was living on Brighton Beach. They all drove luxury cars, had vodka-drinking sprees at birthday parties at tacky restaurants that had names like, *The National*, *Rasputin* and *The Imperial*. Not to mention the beach itself, where men resembled overweight sea lions who would occasionally let out a grunt at their wives, "Rozochka, pass me another sandwich." Their wives were pushing 60, had grandkids, and were still wearing g-strings and letting it all hang out while crunching on sunflower seeds, wearing Gucci sunglasses, and discussing the latest gossip.

I despised that neighborhood, but they had a free beach and the ocean is the same everywhere you go. Vlad was complaining about messy apartment. He wanted me to clean up, and he was being really annoying. I said to Roman, "Yeah, why not, this place is depressing and I can't concentrate on my work anyway. Let's go." I grabbed my swim trunks, and a few beers and we crawled out of our cave to go and find Roman's parked car.

It was July, the middle of the summer. The sun was bright, and the sunglasses were as important as the shoes on your feet. Roman insisted that we take a pull on his joint. Roman was imitating Vlad's complaining, and it was really funny. Roman couldn't remember where his car was parked, so we circled the same block a few times. We were relieved to finally find Roman's car. It was a green sporty SUV. When I looked inside I thought to myself, what a mess. There were CDs all over the dashboard, stickers, circus clothes, empty cans of soda, candy wraps, potato chips and other random objects. After studying my reaction, Roman laughed and asked, "Kind of messy, uh?" – he continued, "Ne ssat'! (Don't piss!) I'll make a space for a you."

Carla and I waited on a bench while Roman was cleaning. He rolled down the windows and put on a CD by this band from the 80's called Akvarium. The song was alright; I didn't think much of it back then. In a few minutes, he cleaned up the space for me to sit in the back. We all got in the car. Roman switched the clutch into the gear and floored the gas pedal. We peeled out of our parking spot, car swerving left and right. I got scared. I never rode through the familiar streets with such speed; it was a very punk rock thing to do. A fuck you finger to the speed limits of the sleepy Kew Gardens. The song was playing, while Roman screamed over it, "This is a classic man! This is the best song ever made! Listen to the lyrics, just listen!" Although it was a quiet song, volume turned all the way up, it definitely ripped through the speakers. The lyrics were, "Ia vizivau Capitana Africaaaa!(I am calling on the captain of Africa)" – strange lyrics, I thought. The singer kept repeating it over and over, until you went into this trance, and then the saxophone solo came on. It was starting to make sense.

Meanwhile, the dude drove like a fucking maniac. This guy had time to do everything: turn his wheel, laugh, smoke, sip a beer, sing, wink at Carla, tell me a joke while I was cursing at the back, "Fuck, watch out!" His car was swerving from left to right, millimeters away from the other cars on the highway. He was drinking a beer behind the wheel. I was sweating and hoping cops wouldn't stop us. I just wanted this car to stop and to get out of it alive.

I made an attempt to cope with it and started drinking my beer in the back seat in big gulps. Carla, on the other hand, was as relaxed as if she was having a conversation with her grandmother. I thought she must have gotten used to his driving skills. I thought that maybe I worry too much and try to control everything; I should just let it go. We made it from Queens to Brighton Beach in record time: 7 minutes! We got out of the car. I was fucking glad we stopped, because my shirt was wet from the heat and stress. All of a sudden it started raining. I was bummed out grumbling to myself, "Great, on top of the fact that we barely made it alive to Brighton Beach, now it's raining and we are not going to get to swim at all. What a waste of a trip!"

Meanwhile, Carla jumped out of the car and started running in circles around the car, getting soaked and yelling, "I am dancing in the rain! I am dancing in the rain!" Roman and I also ran out of the car, and we were all running around the car in this pouring rain. We were stomping on the puddles and getting even more soaked. I forgot all about the driving, and Vlad, and it felt really good to just be silly for a moment. Rain started pouring now. Roman said something to Carla and they started running towards the beach in whatever they were wearing. I was going to question it, but instead I said fuck it and ran after them. As we were getting closer to the water, they started taking their clothes off and throwing them away. Roman and Carla ran into the water already naked. They were swimming and splashing. I looked at them and decided to go in my swimming trunks.

The water ended up being warmer than the rain. It was amazing to swim in this crazy rain. Roman and Carla were about 30 feet from me. They looked like they were making out and enjoying each other in the water. I felt uncomfortable looking at them so I turned around and just continued swimming. It felt great to wash the sweat and stress away. I laid on my back and looked up. Life is good. Rain started coming down harder and harder. I didn't feel like coming out of the water. Roman and Carla swam up to me and Roman asked, "So dude, how are you feeling?" I said, "Great man, but getting kind of hungry." Carla said, "Us too," – and she continued, "Isn't there some cheap Russian food places?" I answered, "Of course, you are in ze Brighton Beach," on purpose sounding very Russian. Roman said, " I am dying for Pelmeni man." (Pelmeni are a Russian type of ravioli.) The hunger drives us all, so we got out of the water and were walking across the beach with wet sand on it. It was a pretty surreal place. Without all the people this was just another beach created by nature.

We found this little Russian restaurant, called Pelmeni House with really great traditional homemade cooking. We ate there, and the food was delicious. After food, we lit our cigarettes, packed in the car and headed back to Queens. On the way back, he was driving a little better, or maybe I stopped minding so much. I was just resting and listening to this great band called Morphine; this time it was my choice. A trio composed of a saxophone, 2 string bass and drums. Smoky, jazzy sounds were filling the space in between our worlds. The cars were lazily passing by and then out of nowhere this long stretch black limo swerved into our lane, like a shark, in front of us from the right side. That was the end of our calm driving.

The Dick Move

Roman noticed an open window at the back of the black limo next to us and he yelled at me, "Dimon, take this bottle of water and give those rich bastards a little shower." I immediately retorted, "Why?" He got mad, "Just shut up and do it," and he was totally serious. I thought it was no big deal, just water, but what if something happened? What if I cause an accident? I protested again, "Nah man, it's too dangerous." He got super serious, as if it was for the survival of the planet. He replied, "What are you, a pussy?" Now I was challenged, and he was really pushy about his stupid wish to demonstrate a divide between the social classes. Once you started calling me a *pussy,* I was pissed. I hated when people called me a pussy. I answered, "All right, you crazy fuck here we go."

I opened the back window of our car that was going 70 miles an hour. He leveled our SUV with the limo, music blasting, and I threw the water from the bottle into their back window. The water from the bottle splashed all over the side of the limo car. The limo driver swerved to the right thinking that another car hit him. Luckily no one was on the right of the limo, so the driver swerved to the left to put his limo back in the lane. The limo driver was furious, rolled down his window and looked like he wanted to jump out of the car. He was yelling something that basically meant, one big long "Fuck You'" and was throwing us a solid middle finger. The limo started gaining on us, I looked at the speedometer, we were going 90 miles an hour. Fuck. Next thing I know the limo driver leveled his car with ours and swerved his wheel to the left to hit our car, Roman foresaw it and swerved his wheel to the left as well avoiding the limo. Great, now we had a speeding limo trying to ram us off the road. Roman was ecstatic, eyes alive and full of excitement. I was pale white and Carla was just calmly smoking.

Limo started slowing down, naturally thinking that they took revenge on us and made us scared, but no, crazy Roman decided to play this cat and mouse game a little more, so he gets in front of the limo and slams on his brakes. Limo driver suspecting what we were about to do also stepped on his brakes. Tires screeched, but luckily no one crashed. I think the limo driver thought that this guy was a crazy fuck and it's not worth wrecking a company car for this idiot so he slowed down. I yelled at Roman, "You fuck face stop doing this stupid shit," lastly Roman shows a middle finger through an open sunroof and speeds away laughing.

Roman was a dick for making us do all that shit just so he could get his kicks. I hated him for that. It was fucked up. I gulped on my beer and tried to feel manly about it. Roman was laughing and yelling, "Did you see his face? Ha! Good one Dimon," as he sipped on his Corona from the cup holder. Cops did not exist for this guy.

We drove back to Queens and I thought to myself, this guy is nuts. I wouldn't want take another trip like that. When we got back, Roman seemed to have made up his mind and he announced to Vlad and I, "We have to go to Virginia to visit Carla's parents for few days." They quickly packed and we said our brief goodbyes. I shook his hand and hugged Carla and told them to drive safely. I was kind of glad to get rid of them and the memory of our psycho drive to Brighton Beach. Somehow I knew that it wasn't the last time I was going to see Roman.

Vlad was happy, and he got back to his usual routine: watching Lord of the Rings and getting stoned. I was thinking to myself, it's nice and peaceful all of a sudden. I was looking forward to some quiet time. I had some work to do, bills to pay and another hangover to recover from. I hadn't seen my parents in a month and felt like I should at least meet up with them for a dinner.

Chapter 5

The Agreement

Dude, I don't want to wear a skirt

The Phone Call

The following Thursday afternoon, I received a phone call from Roman. He sounded energized, yelling into the phone, music really loud in the background. I couldn't hear anything. Finally the music quieted down and I heard him, "Dimon, I am going to California. Do you want to come with me? We are just going to need few hundred bucks for gas and food. What do you say?" He sounded excited.

I asked, "What do you mean? Like a road trip?"

"Yeah, exactly like a road trip. We will have a grand time man. I promise," he sounded pumped.

"Are you going right now?" - I asked.

He said, "No, on Saturday. We are coming back through New York and I have to drop Carla off in Connecticut. But if you want, I can drive through Queens to pick you up first. Let me know soon though. I have to know if you are coming."

I paused and answered, "Nah man. Probably not." I was thinking to myself, "I don't want to be in the same car with him when he drives like a maniac, especially after that last crazy trip to Brighton Beach." I told him, "I don't know. I am kind of busy with work and the band."

He was pushing, "Come on Dimon. Think about this, a road trip. We are going to have crazy fun. This is a once in a lifetime proposal. Think about it and let me know."

I said, "I don't know. I have to go, let's talk later."

"Call me, if you change your mind. Hope you say yes. I need to know soon." He yelled really loud in the receiver, "Byyyyyyyyyye," to make sure my ear hurt. I hung up.

I took a walk to the store to get some food at a local bodega. It was 3 o'clock in the afternoon on a hot mid-summer July. It was only Tuesday. Sweat was forming around my forehead as I walked. I started thinking: sometime in the future I want to go on a road trip, but not now. I can't leave just like this. I wasn't ready. I had things to do. I thought, why is he asking me? He probably just doesn't have the money and I am his way to get to California.

Russian Cougar

I got a call from my Russian cougar girlfriend who was nine years older than me. "Hello Darling, seems to me we haven't seen each other in a while," she giggled, which meant she was ready to meet up to have some fun. She was spoiled, adventurous, full of sexually liberated experiences, divorced once or twice with a shady past of lovers, including her last Italian husband who she still called every other day on the phone and a heroin junkie from the Lower East side. She wanted to meet up and go to some party in Brooklyn. I already knew there would be weird older men and women. They will have a lot to laugh about, and they would be intellectually mind-fucking each other with their smart grown up jokes and patting each other on the ass. I didn't want to go. I knew I would feel awkward and not know where, in the middle of all this do I fit in. She would be the star of the party, and I would be her sidekick that she shows off like a trophy from a hunt.

We were not right for each other. She was an excellent escape artist who was prolonging her own growing up by being with me. She was way too mature for my 22-year-old brain. I was stuck. I knew I shouldn't be with her, but some stupid innocent concept of love deep inside was yearning for the sacrifice of my sanity. I mean of course there were great plusses to her. She was a connoisseur of the exotic food, good music and impeccable taste for anything out of the ordinary. She always knew what she wanted, she was great in bed and she would masturbate a few times a day depending on the music she listened to and the mood she was in.

She knew how to spend all the money we both had to have the best time in New York City. Sometimes we would go for brunch and not leave the place till it was dark and we were broke, but that didn't stop us from going to other places to overdraft our remaining credit cards. I was hopelessly in love with her like a puppy dog in love with a lioness. Her certainty and experience were frightening to me because I felt like all of my inexperienced choices were nothing in comparison to her lavish ones, but I didn't show any of that. I went along. I followed her. I supported her.

She was still on the phone meowing, "Darling you seem distracted, like you are busy or something. Is everything ok with my babuchini?" I remembered how a week before she gave me a stack of poems and said I am breaking up with you. I went to the park, read them, and started crying. I thought my heart was going to break into a million pieces, and the void was growing inside quickly. I didn't want to go to that place where you feel like a miserable used up cloth by the side of the road. I called her back and used my everlasting skill to make everything be all right for the moment, and we made up. I knew that it was a temporary Band-Aid over the gaping void and the heartache that some day would come crushing me like an avalanche, but for now it sufficed and things went back to "normal." I relaxed for a bit after that. I knew how to forget the uncomfortable things rather quickly and just move on in my happy world. I was good at it. I learned from her to be a great escape artist, but she was the best. She was my teacher. We were the best couple to avoid reality together. That's why it was morally and psychologically a fucked up relationship that was eating me up from the inside.

Deciding

A car passed by with windows down and some tacky techno was blasting from the car speakers. God, I hated Queens with all my guts. If I could just figure out a way to get out of here. I was stuck in my choices. Being poor didn't sit well with me, and I loved to travel. I knew how to spend money quickly, but not how to make it last. Being poor and in Queens was a bad combination. I felt like I would never get out. Suddenly, I remembered Roman's offer, and a familiar deep voice within said, "Well, there is your way out." I smiled.

I was scared of Roman, his driving, his way of not giving a fuck about anything. I did give a fuck most of the time. Well, except for when I was drunk, and I was drunk a lot lately. He was even worse than my cougar girlfriend, since she had some sanity and kept a steady job in the city to sponsor her apartment and her lavish tastes for the finer things in life. She at least knew how to make money. Roman had no social obligations, no job, parents that lived somewhere in California and a girlfriend he picked up somewhere on the road. He looked like he was definitely living on a whim of his desires. Of course I didn't focus on all those thoughts. I just felt them. I was aware of them deep down inside, but I didn't consider them seriously. Who cares where Roman is from?

I took off on that road trip thinking "Oh man! A real road trip!" I had only read about road trips but never driven anywhere for more than a few hours. I started thinking of Jack Kerouac's book "On The Road." I imagined what it was like to be on similar adventures. I loved reading books about adventures: the ultimate liberation, the road ahead, and the wheel hugging the white line. I could feel the freedom that he was talking about within reach. Romantic, you might say? Of course I was a romantic, deep inside. We all are romantics! We are just trying to keep busy, acting like robots most of the time. No one had asked me before to go on a road trip. I don't think that many people will, since it takes balls to go across the whole country in a car. Finally, I felt like the decision started forming in my mind, and the more I thought about it the more excitement started to take over. I decided to go, Fuck it! I could use some time away from my weird life. I did not want to think of my next job, how to pay rent, how to satisfy my girlfriend or who to be when I grew up. I just wanted to be free of all those decisions and be driving god knows where, just for the sake of driving.

Fuck Yeah!!!

The same night I called him back and said, "Roman. Let's do it."

He seemed excited, "Awesome, Molodetz!" (Translated from Russian: Ace!).

I added with a serious tone, "But I am not going with you if you are going to drive like that time to Brighton Beach!"

It sounded like the phone dropped, but after shuffling he spoke back into the receiver "Man, I will drive like a grandma. I promise you are going to have the best time of your life." He asked how much money I had in my bank account. I told him I had around four hundred dollars, and Roman thought that it would be more than enough. I asked him what I should take with me. He told me just the basics. We agreed to drive out on Saturday, since it seemed like a good day.

I told Vlad about my idea to take a trip with Roman. Vlad immediately said it was a crazy idea. He told me that Roman was irresponsible, an alcoholic, and a party animal, and gave me a list of other reasons why I shouldn't go, but he knew that I already made up my mind, and his attack as the voice of reason subsided rather quickly. Vlad quickly realized that while I was gone the apartment was going to be all his, so he could probably watch all of his Lord of the Rings movies in one night.

I packed what little I had, and Saturday came rather quickly. Roman and Carla drove in early that morning. I was sitting on the curb smoking, and I heard Roman's car from a block away. All the car windows were down. Some hip-hop music was blasting, and he was rapping along to the lyrics. He pulled up right in front me and said, "What's up Dimon? Are you ready?"

I took a last drag on the cigarette and replied, "Sure." Deep inside, I was still kind of unsure about this trip, but the adventurous spirit got the best of me. Besides, I was looking forward to a change of scenery.

Carla and I went to buy a six-pack for the road while Roman was re-packing the car. When we got back we opened two beers and watched Roman go through the mess in the car. All of a sudden he pulled out two colorful long old ladies' skirts from the trunk and proceeded to put one on. He started dancing around, and then he threw the other one at me.

"Dimon, I decided we are going to go on our road trip wearing skirts." He looked ridiculous.

I protested laughing, "Why? Dude I don't want to wear a skirt."

"Come on, it will be funny. Imagine two grandmas on the road," and he let out a loud belly laugh. I shrugged my shoulders but thought it was a really funny idea, why not? Let the road trip begin!

I put it on and probably looked even more ridiculous than him, but nobody cared. I laughed tripping over the long skirt. We were already a little buzzed from drinking a few beers. The sun was out, and Carla was laughing at us. Roman had finished packing the car and made a place for me in the back. He loaded a CD in with the most appropriate song for the occasion. *Stone Free by* Jimi Hendrix was ripping through the speakers, as we were speeding 70 miles an hour through the quiet streets of Kew Gardens, Queens, leaving sanity in our rear view mirror.

ROAD TRIP STARTS NOW!

Chapter 6

Starting in the Wrong Direction

Becoming teaching assistants

in a sorority house

First Stop – College Town in Connecticut

Roman announced that we had to drive to Connecticut and drop off Carla because she was going to attend summer school in a few days. I thought about it for a moment. That was completely in the opposite direction of where we had to go. I was just about to say something, but then I stopped myself. Who cares? I am already on the road trip. It didn't really matter if we are starting off in the wrong direction as long as we are driving somewhere.

The music was blasting as we drove away from New York. Queens was quickly fading away from my brain like a bad hangover or an unwanted dream from the night before. As I looked ahead, my heart was beating and the cigarettes had never tasted so good. A bottle of beer was in my hand. I lost my fear of drinking in the car and stopped looking for cop cars. They probably had more important things to do.

Roman and Carla were playing some sort of word game, and they were cracking up. I watched them and pondered for a moment: how had those two met anyways? What does she find in Roman, and what does he find in her? I thought it is strange how relationships work. I thought of my weird relationship, but I got a pang in my heart just thinking about it. After a few hours of trying to imagine what the future would bring, I became too tired to think so I just fell asleep in the back seat. As the trees were passing by my half-opened window my eyelids became heavy, and I slid into a dreamless sleep.

It didn't take very long to get to Connecticut. We drove to Carla's neighborhood, and it looked like any other place where white collar, conservative, corporate executives would choose to live. Roman got out of the car to say goodbye to Carla. They walked a little, holding hands. Roman held her head in his rough hands and kissed her forehead. From what I could see, Carla was an antidote to Roman and his internal chaotic fire. Carla resembled a soft feminine river where Roman's turbulent mind could rest. I was thinking they act as if they were together for years, but they just met a week ago. Strange. He kissed her and spoke softly to her. This was the first time I had seen him show any real emotions. When they hugged, her skinny body was lost in his caveman's hug. I laughed to myself a bit; a caveman Roman was wearing a jean skirt. They parted and he came back to the car with a grin.

We waved to Carla as she was watching us pull away. Roman sped up looked over his right shoulder, winked at me and said, "Nu Che (So)...are you ready for the real road trip?"

I replied, "Been ready. Of course, let's do it!!"

Roman slid a CD into the CD Player. It was a song by Eminem, called *White America*. I hated rap and everything about it. At first I protested, in my opinion, the only real music was the kind that had a guitar in it and preferably with a distortion. I didn't like rap, the beats, or the lyrics. Roman listened to my protests for a little while, then looked at me like a father whose patience is running thin and said, "Rule number one: this is my car and I get to choose the music." I was pissed. I didn't like anyone dictating to me how I was going to live, but at the same time his logic made sense.

Instead of rebelling like I always had in the past, I gave in. I asked him why he liked Eminem so much and he said simply, "Just listen to the lyrics man. It's simple. He talks about life man, the street life. He is a white boy who fell in love with street rap. It's brilliant." A joint materialized from his glove compartment, he took a long pull on it and passed it to me. He continued, "I guess we all want to be the opposite of who we are." Here was this Russian mountain climber playing white ghetto boy rap for me. I guess I didn't know the guy at all. He understood it, he identified with it, and the lyrics were ripping through the speakers.

WHITE AMERICA!
I could be one of ya kids,
WHITE AMERICA
little Eric looks just like this,
WHITE AMERICA!
Erica loves my shit;
I go on TRL
Look how many hugs I get.

I looked at the sleepy little Connecticut town we were driving through with their perfect lawns, gardens and driveways. I saw the garages where little kids were getting stoned for the first time. The Eminem lyrics kept on coming through the speakers.

See the problem is I speak to suburban kids
Who otherwise woulda never knew these words exist
These mom's probably woulda never gave 2 squirts of piss
Till I created so much muthafuckin' turbulance
Straight out the tube right into ya livin' rooms I came and kids flipped

Carla walked inside one of those huge houses. She was one of them, a daughter of some VP of some big company with golden letters on his door, and yet she hung out with Roman, who was a law breaking, country crossing, free-loading, hippie immigrant specializing in good times. Opposites attract. I understood that rebellion is a part of liberation, and being an immigrant, I knew what rebellion meant. Ever since I immigrated to the USA, I was fighting hard not to become the cliché of a Russian immigrant. I was rebelling against having limited opportunities, against being put into some stereotype with everyone else, against not being able to speak my mind, against not being able to express myself as an artist.

Now I saw this white-collar neighborhood, *The American Dream* for what it was. Sons and daughters knew their lifestyle was comfortably numb, synthesized, unless they broke out and did something about it and found freedom. That's why some were dropping pills at the clubs, some were running away, some were selling themselves, and some hit the road just to feel real again. For that split second, to be able to close your eyes and say you know what being real feels like. We need rebellion to see where the truth is - to know what the façade is made of and how to disassemble it brick by brick. I felt real sitting in that car. I felt as if I was looking at this ant house from the top. It felt like we were going to create some turbulence and put some holes into their reality. Roman floored that gas pedal and drove off, leaving the suburban houses behind. We flew onto soft streets with huge green trees overhead.

The Prank

He said, "Fuck it. Let's get something to eat!" As we were racing down Connecticut Avenue, I didn't know how we could be doing 110 miles in a 30-mile an hour zone. The streets were wide, and there was lots of space in between the buildings. There were lots of young kids on the streets. It was apparent we were in some kind of a college town. We set out to find a good place to eat. After cruising for a while, we finally parked, and as soon as we got out of the car, we took few photographs with our skirts next to the car. In every one of them we were trying to break a guitar over each other's head, imitating a Spanish Tie style.

Nearby where we parked was this little pizzeria café that had a bar in the back, so we went straight there and ordered a few pints. We were wearing our skirts. He was wearing a baseball hat, and I was wearing a parachute hat and sneakers. We looked pretty ridiculous so we started talking to some people and being our weird selves.

Roman had a knack for attracting listeners with his stories. According to Roman, we were a vagabond Russian circus act traveling from town to town in search of gigs. As the night progressed, the people were getting drunker, and we were entertaining them with more bullshit stories that came from our asses about a hard life on the road as circus performers. We were complaining how there is never a good place to sleep, eat, or even get stoned.

We left the people in the bar thoroughly entertained, drinking and laughing. We went outside, and Roman was just getting warmed up. The beer started kicking in, and we were now talking to some kids outside about the intoxicating effects of performing circus acts. Some college kids, overhearing our conversation, came up to us and, seeing we were having a good time, asked us if we knew where to score a some weed. Roman looked at them, saw inexperienced college freshmen in front of him and said, "Yeah, sure! As a matter of fact, I actually have this awesome dealer in town. We can give him a call right now. Since my dealer is a very paranoid dude, first, give me your money upfront. I will go meet him myself so he won't suspect anything."

The two college kids thought about it for a second and gave him 20 dollars. Roman whipped out his cell phone and started calling some random number intimating that he was asking his dealer for a 20-dollar bag of weed. "Yo Carlos, I got these two kids here, can you drive up through Connecticut Avenue. We are outside of this bar called, " he looked at the name of the place and continued speaking into the phone, "Yeah, aha. It's called the Wild Orchid."

Those kids were thinking yeah we are going to get high tonight. Meanwhile, I could hardly contain my laughter knowing that Roman was a damn good actor and no one is getting high, but I wanted to see how far he would take it. After hanging up the phone Roman told me quietly to meet him around the corner and then pointing at some random car, he yelled, "There he is. He just passed by in his car!"

He told the college kids, "Stay here and wait for me," at the same time winking and nodding his head at me to start moving. I realized that he wanted to take off with their 20 bucks, and I saw a sparkle in his eye - he was getting off on this.

Obviously, the car he was pointing to passed us by quickly without slowing down. The kids soon realized that Roman was trying to take off with their money. They started to make a fuss and yelled, "You are trying to take off with our twenty!" and demanded their money back.

Roman was trying to be even more persuasive. "There! He just passed us! I saw him!" There were bunch of people standing around and beginning to circle us, interested in what was going on. But they already got his trick and they were ready to fight. "Give us back our twenty dollars," they were yelling.

Roman was serious until he realized he was surrounded by people that didn't believe him anymore and there was no more scheming to be done. He said, "Alright, here take your money. It's your choice. Nobody's smoking tonight!" He turned around and started walking away loudly proclaiming that those guys were fools and as we were turning around the corner he started laughing out loud.

"Did you see their faces?" He was enjoying his little scheme.

As we were walking down a well-lit Connecticut Street I asked, "Dude, the phone call was funny, but why did you try to take their money?" - and then Roman looked at me with his childish smile, his little mustache reminded me of some mischievous musketeer.

He said, "Dimon, you have got to understand, it's the most exciting feeling to walk the thin line of what you can do and what you can't do. You take it as far as you can and then when it's not fun anymore you let it go. I didn't want to fight and spoil our good mood. I was just having a little fun. Let's go over there. I have got to piss." The street was way too lit, and the garage he had pointed to looked nice and dark.

"Yeah good idea. I have to piss too."

The Garage Encounter

You can't imagine how amazing it felt to finally piss after consuming 6 pints of beer. As we were relieving ourselves, some guy suddenly opened the door to a nearby house and shouted at us, "Hey you, what the hell are you doing there?"

Roman yelled, "What do you think we are doing?"

I added, "We're pissing."

The guy continued, "Get the fuck outta there!"

I replied, "Hey, let us finish and we'll go."

We were getting really frustrated at this guy's rudeness. Imagine if he was pissing, and I told him to stop and go. He didn't understand how bad we had to go, he was yelling some curse words at us. Roman said, "Pft, this guy is an asshole."

We saw a girl appearing from behind the guy in the doorway, and they started to argue about something. We couldn't figure out whether it was about us or something else. Nevertheless, they sounded like they were fighting. When we were done, we slowly started walking towards them. We were two dudes, obviously not American, both wearing skirts and both kind of drunk. Roman was a pretty fit looking guy with muscles, and I was tall, but no muscles. The guy looked like a confused freshman in college. They clearly were not having a good time. The guy was pissed; he looked at us and started walking fast straight to his car, got inside, rolled down the window and shouted a "Fuck You!" and peeled out with tires spinning loudly.

Roman and I yelled, "Fuck you too," back at him and then we turned around and started stupidly smiling at the girl. We did our darn best to stand straight. It was awkward. We were not really sure what to do next.

She said, "Can you believe that guy?" Her boyfriend or whoever he was had just ditched her. We told her that we thought he was a real jerk and a very rude young man. The girl agreed that he was definitely not a real gentleman. We continued standing and stupidly smiling. We apologized for pissing on her driveway. All of a sudden, I got an urge to have tea. We always had tea with my family when situations got uncomfortable. I thought about asking her if she had any tea. Roman was pulling on his mustache.

I finally asked, "Do you have any tea?" She looked at us and finally noticed our skirts. She started to chuckle into her hand, and then she started laughing louder and louder.

"You guys are such goofballs," and she continued laughing. We looked at each other and started laughing with her. She asks us, "Tea?

Where are you guys from?" We told her that we were from New York and currently we are on a cross-country road trip to California.

She asked, "You don't sound American, where are you from originally?" We told her that we were Russian. She exclaimed, "No way, I have an exam in Russian tomorrow! Oh my god. I suck at Russian. I am going to fail. Would you help me study for it?"

"What a coincidence, we'll help you with anything you need!" we both replied. She gave us a flirtatious look that made my penis turn hard. I looked at her profile. She looked almost like a statue with a bit longer nose than usual.

She asked, "What are your names?"
"I am Dmitry, and he is Roman. And you?"
"Erica. I was born here, but my parents are from Greece."

She motioned to us to follow her and continued exclaiming, "Oh my god, what a coincidence." We chimed in, "Can you believe that?"

We walked inside a 3-floor well-lit brick building. There was a huge flag waving over the entrance to the house with Greek letters on it and then it hit me, we are entering a sorority house! "Ha – lle – lu – jah!" To my college graduate mind, that appeared as a sign sent from the god of lust, wine and rock 'n' roll, Dionysus himself, which promised to be a

70

very good evening. What a weird turn of events. After pissing in this girl's driveway, we end up inside her sorority house. Not bad! Not bad at all!

Adventures at the Sorority House

We noticed it was a bit quiet in the house, so we asked the girl where her roommates were. She explained that they all had finals on the following Monday, and they were studying. Roman replied, "Do they have a Russian exam as well? Maybe they would be needing our help?" He started yelling with a thick Russian accent, "Girls, ver are you? Russians vant to help you study and drink vodka wiz you." The girl laughed at us.

When we got to her room, she asked us if we want to smoke some weed. We exclaimed, "What kind of a question was that? Of course!" We all took a pull on her joint until it was done. We just sat there laughing at each other and at the whole situation that happened 10 minutes ago. Finally, we asked her, what did she want to learn? She fetched a book from her desk with a title "Russian Language 101" and showed it to us. We begged her to read for us and she started reading phrases in a broken Russian, sounding like a 5-year-old girl.

A nice, sweet Greek girl with a big nose trying to read Russian. How fun! I think I got very stoned. Roman announced, "We are nothing without music!"- so he started fumbling with the stereo. After 10 minutes he proclaimed, "I can't figure out how to turn this thing on." I get up walk over to him, and we turn the stereo around. Finally we spot a small power button on the back, and we put on a CD. Music was playing. Some college rock I don't remember. Maybe Weezer.

We were kind of unsure what to do next. Roman said he had to piss and went looking for the bathroom. I looked at the girl with the corner of my eye and saw she was kind of high and she was making herself feel comfortable on the bed. I thought her tight jeans looked real good on her. I pulled up to her and started speaking Russian to her slowly. She looked at me and smiled a little. I really wanted to kiss her. She didn't protest as I leaned over. We started making out, but I kept getting distracted. I felt her nose poking my cheek. Erica was so great at making out if it weren't for her damn nose.

I moved to her neck to get out of the way of the nose and my hands started exploring under her shirt. She had those perfect round breasts, and I couldn't undo the damn bra. She started breathing heavier. I never understood why they created women's bra with this kind of technology for undoing it. Probably to ward off drunken men. They could have created a button or strap, but this was way too complicated of a procedure to perform under pressure. As I was fighting with her bra, I realized I had two things happening in my pants. I had an erection, and I had to piss again. I didn't want to leave her like this, but I had too much beer that night. I couldn't hold it anymore. Oh damn bladder! After I asked her where was the bathroom; I ran in that direction.

Roman was nowhere to be seen. I was waiting for the bathroom, and of course there was some girl taking a shower in the bathroom that didn't come out for a really long time. I started dancing around wondering if I should go outside. I almost pissed all over myself. Finally when the shower stopped, I heard her giggles and a man's deeper voice. I guess she wasn't only showering in there. The girl opened the door with a towel on her head. She apologized for taking so long, smiled and ran to her room. Then none other than Roman comes out after her with a stupid smile, a transparent shower bag over his head and a towel around his waist. He looked wet and very satisfied. He stopped, looked at me and said, "Those showers here – class!" He walked away whistling and straightening his mustache.

I laughed, thinking you lucky bastard, and after I satisfied my basic needs, I ran back to Erica's room. I saw Roman standing in the middle of her room, with a puddle of water all around him pointing at her bed and covering his mouth trying not to laugh. I walked inside the room and saw her sprawled on the bed half-naked, sleeping with a bra in her hands. I guess she gave up waiting on me and fell asleep.

I thought, that's just great, and I had such big plans for her. At that phrase, she started snoring. Goodbye erection! As we stood there trying to figure out what to do next, the snoring got louder. On top of the fact that she had a big schnoz, she was also a snorer. I guess she had a big pull out of that joint. What a quick sorority party that was. I sat down on the bed, and Roman went to get dressed. He came back refreshed and ready to go.

I turned around to Roman and said yawning, "Let's crash here, I am tired."

He replied, "…and do what? Roll around in our sleep from her snoring like a truck driver, or wait till she wakes up? There are still more places to go, things to do, people to see. Plus, I want to get another drink, but first let's see what gifts she has in store for us?"

He started looking around the room and picking up random things from her study desk, while he was repeating a line from a movie, "I don't need anything, maybe just this, and this, and this and that." He grabbed her eye makeup, pack of cigarettes, her Russian book and stuffed those things in his jacket.

At the last motion, my noble feelings for the Greek girl studying the Russian language came up so I protested, "Dude why do you need to take her Russian book? Don't be like that! This girl has a test tomorrow!"

He said," Come on, we'll read it on the road!"

"No Way! Leave the book!" I said angrily.

He saw I was pretty serious, "All right relax, I won't take the book."

He put her book back on the table. We looked at a windowpane, and behind the curtain we saw a 3/4 full a bottle of Grey Goose. Fortune smiled at us. Our twisted Russian hearts tingled looking at the grade A bottle of vodka, which in return glowed back at us in the dim light of the room. We both agreed that it was the best present, so we grabbed the bottle, left our hostess snoring on the bed and went out into the night.

Midnight Zombies

It was the first night of our road trip; we were crossing long Connecticut boulevards diagonally while chugging Grey Goose vodka out of the bottle. As we were passing by some Catholic church, Roman ran up the steps and stood underneath the entrance. With his arms spread apart, as if he was a crucified Christ, he yelled, "Dimon, look! I am Jesus! I am crucified Jesus!"

I answered, "Yeah right, you are more like the Anti-Christ."

Half a block away we saw a black dude walking towards us. He was short and wearing a yellow checker cabbie hat from the 30's. He had a strange goose walk. He was walking towards us and whistling some old tune one usually remembers when it's really late. As he walked closer, we smelled weed. The guy was pulling on a joint.

Roman immediately offered him a bargain, "Hey man, if you got some smoke we'll exchange some Grey Goose vodka for few pulls on your joint." The little guy in a checker hat looked at us and nodded without a word as if he was walking down this way just to hear us say that. The exchange happened as promised. We walked down some dark staircase, and he let us get few drags of his weed and we let him chug some of our vodka. After everyone was satisfied, we had stupid smiles on our faces. We nodded to him and barely made it up the stairs. He walked away the same way he came, whistling the same ol' tune. Suddenly, everything I drank and smoked that night started hitting me all at the same time.

We were walking like zombies. Scattered thoughts, half smiling faces, bodies carried on loose legs, smudged lights, too drunk and high to complete our sentences. Crickets were blasting a cacophony of insect jazz. I turned around and said, "Roooomaaan, thoooseee Criiickkkkeeetsss aaaareeeee soooo looouuuuddd don't yoooou think?"

He turned around and yelled back imitating me, "Yeaaaaaahhhhh theeey aaaaareeeee waaaay toooo loooouuuuddddd innnn myyyy head!"

Then we spotted a pizza parlor on the corner, which seemed like heaven at the end of the train wreck. We walked in, and unable to speak, I raised 2 fingers pointing at the cheese slices and a liter of Coke. Waiting for the pizza took forever. Roman stayed outside talking to some other drunken vagabonds. I gave the pizza guy ten bucks. I couldn't count so I moaned, "Keeep the chaaaaange!" I swallowed those pizzas and chugged the Coke. I felt better.

As we were trekking back to the car, a few homeless bums followed us asking for change, and of course, they picked up the sense of good times coming from our intoxicated auras. We were laughing at them because they were laughing at us stumbling. We were completely wasted and delirious. Those few hobos followed us to the car. I was ready to pass out already, so I went and spread out in the passenger seat, leaving the side door open. Through my half closed eyes and blurry sideways vision, I was witnessing the last event of that night. Roman was asking the homeless to dance for him in exchange for all the coins he had in his car, while he played acoustic guitar and screamed some songs in his wasted drunken voice. While the guitar was cringing under his fingers, he yelled in Russian, "Mama - anarkhia! Papa – stakan portveina!" (Mother – Anarchy! Papa – Glass of Port!) Then he turned towards the dancing homeless and he switched to a ballet conductor role and continued in in English, "Ok girls, and now you jump, and now twirl, and now dance on one foot, and now you turn."

They were dancing very slowly and falling, and getting up again and dancing. He gave them all the money we had by throwing it up in the air singing, "Serebrianyi Dozhd'! Serebrianyi Dozhd'! " (Silver Rain! Silver Rain!) The sun was about to rise, so I closed the car door and put an end to the first day of our road trip.

Chapter 7

Driving Backwards

The hangovers commence

The First Hangover

Roman was already driving when I awoke. It was early morning, and slow music was playing. I couldn't put two and two together. Where was I? I wasn't really sure if he had slept at all or not, but it didn't matter as long as the dude was all right to drive. He looked at me and said, "Good Morning sunshine! Rise and fart!" – and a foul smell followed.

My head hurt, "Ewwww dude, you are such a jerk, I just woke up."
He laughed, "Let's get some coffee for the princess."

We stopped to get coffees and breakfast. We got back on the highway and sped out of Connecticut, back towards New York City. I was hungover. I didn't want to speak. Everything was irritating me. We crossed over to Tappan Zee Bridge to drive through New Jersey and towards Philadelphia so that New York would fade away from our lives. I saw a small green sign on a pole right before we got on the bridge, "*Life is Beautiful.*"

I said to Roman, "That's a nice thing to say to people crossing the bridge."

Roman looked at me and said laughing, "They say that so you don't jump from the bridge, man. Come on!" He looked at me wondering if I really was that naïve. "Oh!" – I said and kept looking out of the window.

We talked about the road plans for a bit. We agreed on one thing at least: we wanted to drive through Florida. We would come down along the coast, through Virginia, North and South Carolina, and stop by Florida to take a swim in the ocean. Then we could stop by New Orleans to hang out there a bit, and then we would continue through Texas, New Mexico, Arizona and finally get to California! Making those plans improved my mood, and things started looking up again. I thought to myself, Life is beautiful. This time without saying it out loud.

Man Skirt

Since we took off from New York, I was wearing the same green skirt with huge white flowers on it. Any lingering ideas about gender segregation were melting away because that skirt was the most comfortable thing to wear. I kept analyzing this phenomenon. Usually men's balls are behind two layers of clothes: underwear and jeans, but in this case, it was only one layer and my man parts were pretty loose and happy. I was kind of digging this newly borrowed fashion. But the visual appearance of this skirt from the outside was suffering; it started to look like a dirty rag, and after inspecting it with my nostrils, I noticed it smelled of beer. I looked at Roman. He wasn't wearing a shirt at all, and he just kept grinning at me through his stupid round sunglasses.

The annoying thing was that he kept changing the CDs because he couldn't find the right song he wanted to listen to. Every song had to be played at the max volume. All the CDs we owned were on the spindles, and all the spindles were on the dashboard. There were about three spindles full of CDs. Every time he would make a sharp turn, those spindles would slide on the dashboard either left or right depending on the turn. Sometimes the turns were really sharp, and they almost flew out of the car since the windows were always open. I had to save the spindles with all our CDs on them in a neurotic game of catch. Sometimes I caught them already flying out of the window. It was a pretty shitty game because if we lost them, all our music would be lost. Regardless, Roman seemed to enjoy this game a lot.

Chapter 8

East Coast Mayhem

"Davai, davai wakey wakey, eggs and bakey!"

The Driving Drunk Party

Californication by the Red Hot Chili Peppers was blasting on full volume. We smoked a bit of the joint that was left over from last night, lit up cigarettes and cracked open a freshly acquired six-pack from the rest area. We drove all morning non-stop through New Jersey and Pennsylvania, and now we were entering Maryland. It was about 4pm. We stopped at the rest area to get another case of beers. Roman walked out of the rest area with a case of Coronas, a pair of new sunglasses, and a hat.

"Nice hat and sunglasses, but why are the tags hanging off of them?" I asked.

He responded smiling, "They were a gift from this wonderful state of Maryland to protect my face and head from this scorching sun!"

It occurred to me, he was also a petty thief. At first I was mad at him, but as I looked back and saw that nobody was chasing after us with sirens and club sticks, I calmed down and got back to my state of mind where everything was groovy.

The sounds were rolling, and the scenery was swaying to guitar solos coming from the speakers. Santana knew how to shred on a guitar his Latin American heritage with a wild percussion in the background. The moon appeared, but it was still sunny. Strange day, I thought, while taking another puff from the joint. I fell asleep for a while and got woken up by thunder. It was raining and our car was swerving seriously from left to right. The empty bottles were clinking on the back seat; my vision was still blurry from sleeping. All I saw was Roman trying to dance while driving.

I screamed over the music, "Dude let's pull over. You are fucking drunk and the car is swerving!"

He yelled, "What!?!?! I can't heaaar yooooouuu!"

I yelled again, this time louder, over the music, "Pull over, we are going to crash!"

He looked back at me, "Awww! The sleeping beauty decides to wake up, and she is scared!" He kept on dancing to some stupid club techno music. I didn't know what to do, but I knew grabbing the wheel from him would be dangerous.

A few moments later, he said, "I gotta piss!"

Continuing to dance, he swerved dramatically to the right, towards a patch of bushes. I heard tires screeching behind us, cars trying to avoid us. I didn't want to look back and see what was going on. Roman drove over the curb, through the grass and straight into the bushes.

He announced, "We are here madam, safe and sound!"

I yelled, "Stop calling me a madam you drunk fuck."

He hiccupped, "Sorry madam won't happen again."

He jumped out of the car, running and yelling, "I am pissing in the rain. I am pissing in the rain." He was pissing and dancing drunk in the rain, laughing, stumbling and falling over his skirt that was getting caught up in his feet. At some point he fell in the mud and stayed there laughing. I really thought he was crazy; I couldn't see or even care what he did. Minutes later, I fell asleep again.

The Music Bonding

The next day, I opened my eyes to sunlight. I leaned back in my seat; the sun was forcing its way into my eyelids. I was fighting it and looked for sunglasses. They were nowhere to be found. I looked at the time. 8:00 am. Roman wasn't in the car. I looked around trying to figure out where we were. My head was hurting. I saw that we were still parked in the same bushes, and the images of last night's drunken driving came back to my mind. Roman came out of the bushes with 2 bags full of groceries. I asked, "Where are we?"

He answered, "In Virginia. I got us a nice six-pack of Coronas and few sandwiches to start the day off right! Davai, davai, wakey wakey, eggs and bakey!" (Davai – Let's go!)

I was rubbing my temples. I wanted to sleep. I took one look at the six-pack and said, "I can't drink anymore! My head hurts."

He answered in the same cheery mood, "Man that's precisely the reason why we shall have few cold ones. The brain needs to stay intoxicated because once you go through a few bottles, you will forget you ever had a hangover." He opened one bottle and started drinking from it. Then he stopped drinking and continued, "All we ever wanted is to start our day, the right way, and they keep pitching their busy lifestyle on us. What if I want to start my day with drinking beer every day? Instead we have to get dressed; get to work, eat your lunch, and go back to work. From work you go home, eat, watch TV, maybe fuck and then go to sleep. To wake up and do it all over again for 30 or 40 more years. Have the damn beer!"

He was getting pissed from his own rant. It was amusing. I sighed and took the beer. A lyric to this 90's song popped into my head, *Ever since the riot all we ever wanted was a black girlfriend!* I decided I needed to hear it to be in a better mood.

"Oh yeah," he interrupted my thoughts. "I have some Tylenol, so you could take that and chase it with some beer. Does your body Grrr-rr-rr-rr-rreat!" We ate the sandwiches and chased them with beers. That bastard was right, my mood started improving a bit, and the sun didn't seem so violent nor did the cars outside of our window. I put on the Cd by Porno for Pyros, and skipped to the song I wanted to hear, "Black Girlfriend" and we started cruising out of the bushes, back on the highway.

Roman was crazy, but I couldn't help admitting to myself that I liked this guy. He was unpredictable, versatile and without limits. The guy was singing:

Ever since the riots
All I really wanted
Was a black girlfriend
They don't play around
They're hard enough
To keep any man in line
Thinking of my pale white skin
Thinking of her dark and smooth
She against me
My black girlfriend.

By the time I finished the second bottle I was already cheery like Roman, and we started singing together:

Ever since the riots
All I really wanted
Was a black girlfrieeeend.
She against me
My black girlfriend.

Cursing, laughing loudly, with cigarettes in our mouths and music blasting, we drove onwards. Porno For Pyros was replaced by one of my personal favorite bands, *Auktyon*. If there was a name for the style of music this band played, it would probably be called Russian avant-garde, indie, jazz, folk rock. They were shamans on the backdrop of Russian Soviet Perestroika of The Eighties. They used to have a ballet dancer on stage while the band was playing. The showman, *Garkusha* (named after a stuffed crow, a character in a children's TV show), in a hip black suit, black eyeliner and a suitcase full of weird little instruments, would read experimental poetry in between the songs. The leader of the band would hide behind *Garkusha* and would leave planet Earth for the duration of the bands performance, only occasionally opening his eyes to check the guitar tuning. The song that was playing was called, "The Hunter." The music was written in a major chord progression, but the lyrics were completely the opposite, as if it was some kind of a sonic invocation for the dead.

Down the river, oars in the sand,
remember the lesson,
about the red hunter,
he is a dead hunter
aiming at the dead only.
After he shoots, the river
rests come to the brook,
in the city of the dead at night,
the hunter will give us a weapon,

targets for hunting are the lights of the night.
I became the shooter,
the hunter shoots at me as well.
Now we are shadows, we are alive.
Hunter look for me, binds me down,
look for me the hunter of fire.

After that CD was done, we decided to continue in the same fashion, but take it up a notch.

Amongst the very few belongings I packed with me, I found Gogol Bordello "Voi-La Intruder" in my bag, and that was the beginning of our intruding into the lives of people we met. Gogol Bordello, whose lead singer is Ukrainian-born Eugene Hutz, has a special knack for injecting your brain with grenades of complete disorder and mayhem with fierce gypsy punk, violins, accordions, and saxophones. My cougar ex-girlfriend introduced me to his music. It could be compared to being on a train full of drunken gypsies that was going off rails and falling off a bridge, all while having the best time of your life dancing to thundering disco beats and endless gypsy violin solos. Gogol Bordello was rapidly making its way into our brains with its thirst for chaos.

Cutting Down Pirate's Booty

I put some pilot's goggles on, and Roman impulsively rolls into some random parking lot. To the right, I saw three flags swaying in the wind: one Canadian, one British, and one Australian. Looking at these flags, Roman said to me in a serious tone, "Let's steal those 3 flags."

I protested. "How? They are huge, they must be bolted to the floor!"

"Ne ssat'! (Don't piss!) I have a plan," he exclaimed.

Here was his plan: I had to go to the store and ask the people for directions. Meanwhile, he would pull over and park his car with the open trunk blocking the flags. Then, by his signal, we axe down the flags and put them in our trunk. He was beaming at me as he asked with his hands open, "How do you like my plan?"

I listened to his plan almost in disbelief, since it was a totally stupid and crazy idea. Although, looking at him I saw that he was totally serious about it. I said, "Fuck it, let's do it!"

I had one last question,

"Wait, but how are we going to axe them down?"

He leaned over and whispered in my ear,

"I have an axe in my trunk."

I didn't believe him. "You are lying," I said.

He went to the trunk and after searching for a while he whipped out this huge wood cutting rustic looking axe. I was in awe. He was the all time collector of random bullshit items; that's for sure. Now we had all the tools. It was time to act.

I went to the store to ask for directions. With wide-open innocent eyes, I was pretending to be a lost driver looking for the road to Florida. The place ended up not being the rest area that we thought initially, but a travel agency, which explained the flags swaying in the wind. Waiting in line after me was a family with this pretty cute sixteen-year-old girl who was looking at me with those huge questioning eyes. I think I was still wearing a skirt. The travel agent lady politely explained to me how to get to Florida. As I was leaving I winked at the 16 year old, who blushed and looked away. I went outside and Action! Everything happened according to the plan, as if we were thieves stealing a large rare diamond from a high security bank. I ran to the car, grabbed the axe and went to work. While Roman held the flags, I axed the British, Australian, and then the Canadian one. They went down like Christmas trees in the middle of the summer. We threw them in the trunk, jumped in the car and drove away as fast as we could.

Getting back on the highway, we were really satisfied with ourselves. Feeling like pirates with the booty in the trunk, we celebrated by opening fresh beers. I didn't know why we needed flags, but we cut them down anyways. I was entertaining the idea of the people at the travel agency finding out about their flags being cut down. How long would it take them realize that? Would they suddenly see it? Would they remember a month later? I would have given 20 bucks to videotape their faces. Ha! A few hours later, we finished that six pack, and I was feeling kind of buzzed already. We decided to make a pit stop to restock on the drinks.

"What's the problem, Officer?"

We rolled into this rest area that looked like any other rest area, and as we got out of the car, or more like, fell out of the car with beer bottles in our hands, we noticed people looking at us from a nearby car as if we had fallen from an alien ship. We went in, found the restrooms, and another idea overtook our drunken heads. He grabbed a bathroom mop and began throwing water all over the floor as if he was a janitor. Meanwhile, I opened all the faucets and let the water run. We started a water fight by directing the streams of water at each other from the different corners of the room. In about five minutes, the water was filling the room quickly. It started flowing towards the door in waves.

We ran out of there, yelling and splashing water everywhere, bought some cigarettes and more beer, and ran back to the car. Right before we got into the car, we uncorked two of the beers and started pounding them. A car parked next to us had kids inside pointing at us, asking their parents what we were doing. The parents prohibited them from opening the doors and drove out to park somewhere else. We jumped into the car, music blasting, and pulled out from the parking lot. We wished everyone to have a great fucking South Carolina day, and after throwing few empty bottles out of our windows, we got back on the highway.

Five minutes later Roman said to me, "Dimon, collect the empty bottles and throw them in the back quickly." He sounded pretty serious.

I asked him, "What's up?"

"We got cops behind us!"

I looked back and saw a cop car with sirens wailing. I said, "Shit! We are drunk!"

Roman looked at me and snapped, "Just chill the fuck out, we'll be alright. Ne ssat'! (Don't piss!) I will take care of it".

He jammed four sticks of gum in his mouth. I was panicking big time, but I climbed over to the back and cleaned out all the empty bottles. We pulled over. The cop parked behind us. The officer came around to the driver's side, looked inside inquiringly, his hand on his gun holster, and asked us to see some papers. Roman calmly handed him license and registration, and with the biggest grin he proceeded to ask, "What is the problem officer?"

Officer looked over his license and said, "Some folks from the rest area reported misconduct back there. "

We looked at each other with really surprised faces, "We haven't heard of any misconduct officer."

"Why then, did they say it was two guys in a green Nissan Exterra wearing women's skirts?"

We knew we were fucked.

"You been drinking?" Officer inquired.

We answered, "Of course not," trying not to breathe.

It was a decisive point of our journey; we had to come up with something quick. Roman looked at the officer, and in his most sincere tone delivered a speech, "Dear Mr. Officer, I know that people back at that rest area might disagree with our lifestyle, but we are free hippies travelling to California. I have been to New York, and now I am travelling back with my friend." The cop looked at me, and I waved at him with a stupid smile. Roman continued, "We haven't done anything wrong. Look at us officer, we are simply wearing skirts, and on my license plate it says Sunny State of California. To those people at the rest area, anything we do already seems inappropriate. Just because we like to wear skirts, they already judge us. They think we are some crazy homosexuals or something like that, but we just like freedom from our pants and underwear. As a matter of fact, in California many people don't wear pants anymore."

I am thinking to myself, "What? That's it we are totally fucked." Those moments of silence were treacherous and long. They seemed like an eternity. My foot jerked. The glass bottle clinked under my foot. I started sweating, hoping he didn't see that. Looking down under my seat, I saw a beer bottle sticking out. Luckily, next to it there was a Snapple bottle. I quickly picked it up and showed it to the cop. To disarm his look of doubt, I took a sip from it. It tasted like ash from cigarettes. Earlier, we were throwing our cigarette butts in that bottle of Snapple. I gulped the juice and swallowed it with a very hard to come by smile. The cop looked inside again. My cleaning worked. The back seat looked immaculate. I stuffed all the shit far under the seats. I did notice one thing I forgot to put away: huge brown ladies underwear. The cop looked at our skirts and then at us again. I gave him the sincerest smile, and the cop made a grimace. He didn't want to go into asking more questions about the liberal Californian hippies who didn't wear underwear.

To my biggest surprise, the cop returned the license and registration to Roman and said, "Get out of my state ya' hear. Otherwise, I will be right there when you decide to mess with my state property again," and he walked away. We pulled out and started driving away very slowly. I was half-choking on that sip from that Snapple bottle, but I was so glad that we got away clean. That scene was the turning point that nominated Roman all-time star of bullshit stories.

I was yelling and clapping, "Fuck yeah, I can't believe that worked. You are a genius bullshitter!"

He was grinning back at me and exhaling with a relief. He added, "It is true." He looked at me from under his sunglasses and continued, "We are pantsless hippies going to California. Pass me that Corona."

I was thinking to myself, we are so damn lucky. We almost got arrested for that shit at the rest area bathroom. That night we decided to clean up our act, so we drove until it was dark. Then it began to rain. We got off on the exit and parked somewhere. Last thing I remember was falling asleep in the car with rain pounding on the roof.

Pee Dee River

In the morning, I opened my eyes and found us parked in a very random place. Light raindrops were falling on the windshield, making a soothing sound, which reminded me of my family's country house in Moscow. We would sit around a large kitchen table, all 4 of us, and light rain would be falling on the roof while my grandmother was preparing a warm breakfast for us. An abundance of raindrops created little rivers on his windshield. There were no cars around us anywhere in sight. I just saw grass, trees, and a river about 20 feet to the right.

"Hey Roman? Ti gde? (Where are you?)" There was no answer. I called again. No answer, but something started moving on the roof. I thought it was an animal that jumped on the roof. I freaked out and jumped out of the car quick. When I looked up I saw that we were parked under a bridge next to the river. Roman was sleeping on the roof of the car inside his sleeping bag. I thought, I guess it's like camping.

He woke up immediately, got out of his sleeping bag and jumped down from the roof. "Let's go for a swim," he said with a mischievous smile.

I read the sign with the name of the river, Pee Dee River, North Carolina. "Sure, let's go swim in Pee Dee River, ha ha ha!"

Washing ourselves in the river with the light rain coming down felt like a baptism. It was a really sweet spot. Huge green tree branches hung over the river that was flowing towards an ocean. I thought, how many more rivers flowed towards an ocean, where do all these rivers start? The river was about 100 feet in width and the water was cool and refreshing. We were bathing our dirty, smelly bodies from yesterday's debauchery. When I got out of the car, I thought a fire would complete the picture. I gathered a few logs and even though they were a bit wet from the rain, I still managed to make a little fire under the bridge next to the car to warm us up. Roman sat next to the fire as well, lit a cigarette and stared at it for a while. The red glow was mesmerizing. We didn't speak. It was really cool just to stare at it.

After a long pause he said, "Fire can burn anything down, but water is stronger than the fire. Fire needs a spark, and water needs nothing. It just flows. It's a law of nature my man, and you can't fuck with nature."

He stared at it long and without interruption and then he continued, "You have to live your life intensely, and be a spark and burn, burn, burn man, because one day the water will put out your fire and will take your ashes to the big ocean."

Those words hung in the air for a while, as the sounds of the river were creating a sonic backdrop for this perfect moment. I didn't feel like leaving, but young blood has to keep moving on to the next adventure. We put out the fire and got back on the road.

Penniless Optimism

As we were getting back on the road, the sun crawled out from behind the clouds and sprinkled gold upon its surroundings. The car was gaining speed, and we passed a road sign that said South Carolina. Roman found a roach, left over from the few days ago, and we smoked it carefully, holding it with medical tweezers. We opened few fresh bottles of beer and stared at the road in front of us while listening to some 60's reggae music. A few hours later, it got really hot, so we drove into a rest area. We just ran inside to get a cold drink. I wanted to use the restroom first, but Roman got there before me and locked himself in there. He wouldn't come out for 20 minutes, so I started knocking on the door. I had to go real bad. I started banging on the door, "Come on dude, get out, I gotta go!"

After knocking for a while the door all of a sudden opened and I fell inside. The light went out and I got hit over the head with something that shattered. I heard glass falling on the floor. I turn around and saw him holding a painting that had a glass cover on it, luckily for me he hit me with the side that didn't have the glass on it, but nevertheless the glass splattered all over the room. He was laughing.

I completely lost it and I started yelling at him, "What the fuck dude! You think that's funny?" and started punching him. He ran out, and I ran after him.

I heard cursing in our direction from the Indian guy behind the counter, "You broke my restroom! You broke my restroom. You pay for it! I call the police! I call the police!"

We ran outside, I put my wallet on the roof of the car and put on my t-shirt quickly. We got in the car and drove away as fast as we could before the guy called the cops. I checked my back for injuries and saw there was none but a small bump on my head. I was relieved but still pissed and angry. I didn't understand those kinds of jokes. He was having a grand old time though, pissing me off.

I said, "Stop at the Burger King." He got off at the next exit. We went inside Burger King and as I got ready to pay, I realized I didn't have my wallet. Fuck! I looked everywhere. I start remembering the events that took place before we got here. When we ran out of the rest room, I placed my wallet on top of the car to put my shirt on. We jumped in the car, and I left my wallet on the roof. Damn! Fucking Shit! That was stupid. Our money was running out, and now we were really screwed. Roman could probably survive in the jungle without food, since he would make friends with the local monkeys and steal bananas from them.

I was pissed at Roman, "What the fuck did you have to do that for? Dude now we have no money!" He was imitating me and laughing instead of thinking seriously. There was nothing else to do. I had to eat my pride and turn around and go back to the same rest area. I put on a different shirt and shorts, to avoid being recognized. "Stop your stupid laughter and drive me back," he was really enjoying looking at me being angry.

Trying to slide by the guy at the counter, I ran to check the restroom for my wallet, but it was locked and there was a sign on the door, "Out of Order" The guy that was working the counter, looked at me, recognized me and started yelling, "You broke my restroom! You will pay for it!" He was advancing towards me. I ran outside. As I ran I searched the floor with my eyes, nothing.

Roman picked me up and we drove off real quick. We searched the route back to the highway. Roman was driving slowly, and I was searching for it. Our little bathroom trick ended with us losing all of our money, or more like my money, since he only owned a car with bunch of crap in it. We were fucked. I started getting stressed out. Being hungover for the last 5 days without good sleep started to take a toll on me. On top of it all, I knew that I was pretty close to zero on my account anyway, so something had to be done.

I was really hungry, so we decided to go back to that Burger King to figure out what do next. We collected the change we had in the car: enough to buy two cheeseburgers and fries. That uncomfortable feeling when you are counting change while you got people waiting in line behind you made me feel depressed inside. We went outside to eat on the hood of our car. I stood there chewing the first bite of that burger and chasing it with fries. It was the best tasting burger ever. Roman, a fuckhead without brakes, decided to have a food fight with our last two burgers and French fries. He grabbed my burger and started running away. I ran after him and he turned around and threw it at my face, so I yelled "you are such an asshole" and he ran away like a 5 year old. Man I was so mad, and he was acting like we didn't just end up throwing away our last food. I was hungry.

Thoughts started creeping in on me. I was getting tired of this immature asshole, he was getting on my nerves. It seemed as if he was pushing my buttons to get a kick out of it, trying to see how far he could take it with me. I wanted to beat the shit out of him because he was annoying the hell out of me. I went back and sat on the curb. He was having too much fun at my expense. He came back and sat next to me on the curb.

He patted me on the shoulder and as he opened his mouth burger pieces flew at me as he said in a joking voice, "Come on man, don't be so serious. Ha ha ha! We can go collect the leftovers somewhere over there. Ha ha ha! It was fun though, right?"

I looked at him. I couldn't believe what he was saying. I replied, "Dude are you really stupid or you are just pretending? You threw away our last food, that was our last money and I am hungry."

I pushed him back off the curb. He fell off still laughing. Although I was freaking out, I tried to calm down and thought for a second of our options.

Meanwhile, he started imitating me, "Oh, my god, Mommy listen to this baby. He has got no food and he is going to starve to death! Somebody throw him a quarter."

He was really crossing that line with me and I thought what the hell was I doing here with this idiot? It was a mistake driving with this asshole. I got up and started packing my things in the car.

He asked me, "What are you doing?"

I replied, "What do you think I am doing? Going home."

He got up quickly, "What the fuck is wrong with you, Dimon." He got serious, "Have you never been without money, food and nowhere to go? I am asking you. You are used to having everything served on a platter for you. Well guess what! Life is not like that, sometimes you end up in deep shit, and you still gotta have some fun, because all the other people think how much money they have or will have or will not have tomorrow and they forget that all we have is today, right now and tomorrow is a big joke. What are you going do now without money? You big sissy! Live it up man, and live it in. Think and you will figure it out, but don't let that define you. Don't let the lack of money define you and affect your emotions, your outlook on life, or how much fun you can have. Because the only thing that is real, when you don't care about fucking money, but you are being yourself – that is the only way out of this madness. You hear me?" His eyes were wild and crazy.

His screwed up wisdom was making sense, but I was still hungry and pissed off. He was right in a way: I was overreacting. I was forgetting that we still had the car and gas in it, and music and that we would come up with something. "All right, I get it, I am just too damn hungover to be having fun."

I went back to the car to get a cigarette and saw my driver's license on the dashboard, since we had to show it to the cop who stopped us. I lit up a cigarette and thought about it for a moment. There comes a time when you think of places and people that can help you to score some money, and slowly you start realizing that your parents are the only ones that can help you out. I wasn't on the best terms with my family at that time, since they hated my crazy ex, but I could always count on them in hard times, since they were my parents, after all, and no matter how much I rebelled, I knew they were always there for me.

I thought of the worst criminals who tattooed words like "I Love Mom" or "Mom Forever" on their arms. I thought of Henry Miller struggling in Bushwick, Brooklyn as a writer, asking his parents for money as a grown man, and thought I could ask my ever-giving mom for few hundred bucks until I got back from this road trip. We drove to the phone booth, and I called my mother. It was nice to hear her; moms always know how to make you feel good. They also know really well how to harass you with questions.

After her endless exclamations, and my assurances that we had a place to sleep and everything was great, I told her about losing my wallet. I told her that I needed a few hundred bucks and asked her to wire money to the local Western Union. She understood and agreed as long as I promised to call her more often. I assured her that I would call her every day and went to Western Union to wait for the money. Finally after a long pause cashier gave me three hundred dollars and a receipt. When we got it, I was relieved, and my mood started picking up. I decided to be responsible, and to celebrate a little bit by buying ice cream and sandwiches.

We were munching on ice creams as we were getting back on the highway towards Florida. Now we had money to fund our adventures and gas for the car. Life was good again, but of course we didn't learn any lessons, otherwise I wouldn't be writing this story. We started spending the money right away. Music was blasting. A new CD was playing, and we were grooving to all-time college favorites, perfect accompaniment for anyone who wants to be irresponsible.

Exits are for those who want to exit. We just want to piss!

We decided that day to have a little excursion into one of the towns we were passing through, deep in South Carolina. We stopped at some random parking lot, got out of the car, and went to get something to eat. We walked down the line of stores adjacent to the parking lot, and walked into a barbershop. I didn't know why we went in there, but we did. People were looking at us rather surprised. We looked like road tripping she-males: tall burly dudes, wearing skirts, smelling of fire, looking really odd, and speaking with Russian accents. Roman grabbed a can with a hair coloring solution, and started asking the barbers that worked there about the effects it had on hair. The color was red, so I was looking at him wondering, "What the hell does he need a red color for?" Being with him for few days on the road, I knew there must have been a reason, since there was a reason for having an axe and flags in the car. After his numerous questions, he flashed them one of his famous *I am a lucky bastard and I can get away with anything* smiles, said goodbye to everyone and left. Everyone exhaled with relief. As he was leaving, nobody saw in the crowded hair salon how he slipped the hair-coloring bottle into his shorts and walked out.

We got back in the car and started driving with fresh beer bottles in our hands. This time we were drinking in moderation. In a few hours, I wanted to piss badly, so I told him dude, "Let's get off on the next exit."

He said to me, "Exits are for those who want to exit, we just want to piss!" and swerved his wheel to the right.

I closed my eyes to not see. I hated this tactic. We swerved into an open field with tall bushes all around. I was cursing him out; he was just excusing himself, "When one has got to piss, one needs to piss!" When we came to a sudden stop, he left the car on and ran about 10 feet away towards the bushes. Then I heard the long satisfactory exhale of an accomplishment, right as he was receiving a phone call on his cell phone. To my surprise, it was a call from Moscow from one of his flings. He started speaking Russian and I couldn't tell if it was another one of his girlfriends, wives, one-night stands, or their mothers, since he found a common language with women of all ages and they all loved him dearly.

"Solhishko, kak dela?
Nu ia po tebe tozhu skuchal. Tak rad tebya slishat!"
(Darling, how are you?
I missed you too. I am glad to hear from you as well.)

As he was shaking the last drop off of his wiener,

"Gde ia? Ia v Uzhnoi Karoline, posredi Ameriki!"
(Where am I? I am in South Carolina, in the middle of America.)

From what I overheard, he was telling her that we are on the road right now, traveling cross-country, and how little she knew how much he missed her and that the world became so technologically advanced that you can talk to someone while you are pissing. He was laughing and having a jolly time. I was looking at him with disbelief. He had time for everything; too bad he didn't have a third arm, he would have been driving too.

Improving Our Appearance

He came back with elevated spirits, whipped out a can from his pocket with the red coloring solution and said to me, "This is a perfect time to take care of our appearances. Let's color our hair!"

I asked, "Now?"

"Yeah, what's wrong with now?" He retorted.

I shrugged my shoulders. I guess nothing. We poured water on our hair and then sprayed red color all over it and then waited for the color to kick in. In 10 minutes, I looked in the mirror and thought I looked like a strange leopard that had one black line and one red all around my head. It was stupid, but kind of weird and cool at the same time. The more I looked at myself, the more I thought something was missing and I realized I never had an earring, but always wanted one.

I told him about the missing detail in my appearance. He said, "Net problem (No Problem), we will pierce your ear right now!"

I asked, "How? Don't you need a piercing machine for that?"

Roman reassured me, "Nah, don't worry, it will be very quick. I have just the perfect earring for your sweet face." I always wanted to pierce my ear.

He whipped out an earring from his glove compartment and a little bottle of perfume and sprayed some on my earring. He winked at me, made the music louder as he was holding my left ear with one hand he slammed the earring into my earlobe with another hand. I yelled, but it was already in my ear. My virgin ear got pierced right there and then, and the earring was none other than a golden Native American feather. I thought that was a big honor, so we were pleased with our make over and decided to keep on driving. We drove out of the bushes and got back on the highway. The blood from my ear was trickling down my neck and I was occasionally wiping it. He reassured me, "Don't worry it'll heal before you get married, ha ha!" – one of the famous Russian sayings. I laughed. I didn't mind. It stung a bit, but I was proud to have my ear pierced in such a punk rock way without any shiny studs.

Pill Popping Truck Driver Party

Later that day, I took over the wheel and was driving with all the attributes of a Native American chief: feather in my hair and an earring in my ear. We stopped at the rest area to get a drink. At the counter I saw a pack of pills that read, *Energy Pill To Stay Awake for 8 hours*.

My brain started thinking that little pack must have some kind of interesting kick to it, like Ephedrine, which was in every Advil pill. I learned one thing: when you stay up late and go to work in the morning, Advil Cold and Sinus pills were the best hangover medicine. They gave you that necessary kick in the morning to get your head working that coffee couldn't do. I thought I could finally find a cure for this week long hangover.

A peculiar story came to mind by this Russian psychedelic fiction writer, Victor Pelevin, who introduced the Russians in the 90s to acid, ephedrine and psychedelics. The story was called, *The Crystal World*

In this story two White Army cadets (White Army – army of nobility, as opposing to Red Army – army of communists) had to keep watch for a communist leader looking to sneak into the *Smolni* (Occupied Headquarters of the Red Army) through the small alley they were guarding. As the hour was getting late and the young cadets were getting bored they started sniffing a little white powder to keep awake. The writer tells us that white powder was pure ephedrine, which is stronger than cocaine. The two cadets got really high forgetting their purpose there and instead, they were enjoying their philosophical discussions about life and purpose. Strange characters trying to get into the alley they were guarding constantly interrupted them, so they had to patrol from time to time, but they carried on their observations. One cadet told his companion he foresaw his mission in life, to not let an ancient demon destroy an empire. They were much entertained by this conversation. Eventually they saw a short odd-looking man in a long coat with a goatee coming their way wearing a civilian cabbie hat, a mustache and a beard.

When he came up to them they yelled out, "Who goes there?" He started explaining. He said his name was Eino Rankhaia, and he had to get the delivery of lemonade into *Smolni*. They discovered that he had a really strange speech impediment. He was using the G-sound to replace the R-sound, which came out very funny. Instead of Dear Sirs, he said Deag Sigs. They thought he was the funniest character they came across. They laughed mispronouncing the letters back at each other while they kept sniffing some ephedrine. They even offered some to the short man, but he declined and said he had an urgent matter to attend. The cadets were in elevated spirits so they wished him to have a warm night and to come back through the same alley to make them laugh again. That odd-looking short man ended up being the head of the communist party: Lenin himself. Apparently that cadet failed his mission in life and allowed the empire to be destroyed by an ancient demon that brought Communism to Russia.

Spending a little more time contemplating the effects of those pills, I decided to experience it firsthand. I came back to the car. Roman was snoring through his hangover. I looked at those pills and decided to try the whole packet for that extra kick since my mission probably had nothing to do with an ancient demon, or did it? I got behind the wheel and started driving. Although I was a horrible stick shift driver, I could do alright on an open road.

Twenty minutes later, it came like a rush to my head. Concentration on any object in my vision got really intense. I felt as if I was a cobra that just spotted a mouse. That's how sharp my vision got. My hands were getting sweaty as I held the steering wheel really tight. I felt my body becoming lighter and emanating warmth. The cigarette in my mouth all of a sudden became the tastiest thing in the world. I focused on the red lights of the car in front of me. Every time I inhaled the smoke it went really deep into my lungs. When I exhaled I watched the smoke in front of me curl slowly. The music was made of rhythmic patterns, notes, vocal melodies and different frequencies that were all coming down on me like Niagara Falls. I wanted to swim in music. The driving got easier, and I felt as if I was driving a ship on wheels with my pinky finger.

I thought about my attitude towards the whole trip and how uptight I had been and how I hadn't relaxed since we took off. I started feeling as if I was driving this big truck on a long distance haul from all those 80's movies. I put on my baseball hat to top things off, and I was a truck driver from a Sylvester Stallone movie chewing on a cigarette.

Roman climbed out of the coat he was covered with and looked at me, trying to figure out what's going on. I was rocking out like a madman and chewing on my jaw, he mumbled, "Don't tell me you took some energy pills!"

I yelled back, "Hell yeah! Man if you take two of them it has a nice kick to it. I have another packet you wanna try?!"

He said, "Oh oh, I will give you 30 minutes until you crash."

I answered, "Shut up man, I will be fine."

My eyeballs were the size of nice round silver dollars with dead presidents on them and I was grinding my teeth really loud. The next song came on and it was System of a Down, and I was yelling, "*Fuck the system, Fuck the System*", then I put on good old Ramones, "*Sheena was a punk rocker*" and soon the Rolling Stones were yelling, "*And if you meet me have some sympathy and grace!*" That was my kind of music and it spoke to me like no other human being could.

It felt good for the next half hour and then some metal music came on and lizards and rats started crawling out of the speakers. I turned the music off. I started getting tired. The sun was setting, my little party was coming to an end, my airplane was descending pretty damn fast and things were starting to get on my nerves. The first thing that irritated me was the shower I hadn't taken in a long time and that I was starting to smell like a bum. I started thinking that Roman was right about me crashing, but I didn't want to accept it, so I started swearing back at him for no apparent reason, "You are so full of shit. Fuck you and your freaking wisdom! You always try to make me feel bad." He was just sleeping through it all. In about twenty minutes, I felt nauseated. We had to get off the highway, and in about 5 more minutes, I was standing in front of the headlights of our car and puking whatever was left of the sandwiches I had a few hours ago. Roman woke up and sat there looking at me. "Told ya Ninja, don't overdo it," I mumbled, "Shut up," and climbed inside. "Guess it's my turn now." He smirked and took over the wheel. I felt shitty so I went back to sleep on the back seat. Soon we'd be there. Ahhh, FLORIDA!

Chapter 9

Florida Decadence

The Russian roulette with punches

or

Defending the honor of wearing

European Swimming Trunks

In All Our Glory

The next morning we were cruising down the highway and around noon we drove into the state of Florida – the perfect place to have some freaky American fun. We decided not to drive all the way to Miami Beach and to just stop by the closest resort town in Florida where we could swim and kick back for few days. On the map, Panama City seemed like it was the closest to Route 10, which we were planning on taking all the way to New Orleans, so we decided to go there. The sun was shining. We started seeing occasional palm trees, and our mood was improving.

As we drove into Panama City, Roman had an ingenious idea that it was time to let our international ship on wheels cruise down Main Avenue with the appropriate attributes. We put Black Sabbath in the CD player and pulled out all our stolen flags from the trunk and hung them out of our car windows; Canadian from the right passenger's window, Australian from the left, and the British one stuck out of our sunroof. It was quite a spectacle. We looked like we were headlining a procession for a racing car competition. We were laughing and shouting, and people were pointing at us and shouting back. I finally realized why we had to axe those flags down and I was proud of Roman's planning skills.

Sporty convertibles everywhere, bad techno music blasting, Jeep Wranglers with girls hanging out of them, and surfer dudes with their boogie boards. Some girls were wearing bikinis, so we screamed some random things at them, praising god for creating women in such fine shapes and forms. As the trees cleared on the right, we finally saw a sandy beach and ocean waves breaking. It was getting hotter and hotter, and we wanted to swim badly.

When we got to the beach we parked our car and ran to the water. After living without a shower any chance to swim in the water gets you closer to heaven. We jumped into that blue and green water splashing and yelling. Naturally, there were only few people on the beach. I remembered that it was Thursday noon, and normal people were probably working in white, air-conditioned offices wishing they could go for a swim. Meanwhile, we were swimming to our hearts' content. I thought to myself: "Ahhhh, the freedom to do whatever you want." Now I knew how it felt to be on the road. We were baptized, born again, refreshed and ready to drive to the edge of the world.

As we got out, we looked for food and decided to have a feast, so we headed to the Mexican place a few blocks away. Those tacos were the meaning of life. They were the reason for breathing and waking up in the morning. It doesn't get better than to wash tacos down with a few Coronas. We had officially made it in life.

Asshole

Meanwhile, reality kicked in; our money was running low again. We had spent the last few hundred my mother wired me, and I was getting worried again. The same thoughts kept repeating until my head hurt. What's next? How are we going to get to California without any money? We were cruising around looking for something to do next. It was getting dark; the dark matters were brooding over our heads, since we are after all creations of good and evil, dark and light, black and white. This time the vicious moods of denial, paranoia, and revenge triggered Roman. The darkness surfaced and dry sarcasm seeped out of him like venom.

He was making fun of me, "What are you going to call your mommy again ha?"

I fought back, "Dude what the fuck? That's enough. Whose money are we spending right now since you don't have shit of your own?"

He kept on, "OOOOhhhh poor baby," and it turned into making fun of my music. "What the fuck is this are we listening to? This eighties bullshit is getting on my nerves."

I was thinking; here we go again. What am I doing here, I am not sure anymore. He had serious mood swings; one minute all is well, the next minute all hell breaks loose. I was realizing more and more my friend over here is completely bi-polar. This time he bulldozed over my line and I was fed up,

"That's it I am taking off! Fuck this stupid road trip! I don't need to take crap from you anymore!"

He replied, "What are you going to do about it?"
I responded, "Fuck you man!" I am just going to get my shit and get the hell out of here and get on a plane back!"

He exploded back, "I am getting sick and tired with you telling me what the fuck we should do!"

I was fighting back. I was getting angrier. He was pissing me off, and I wanted to punch him.

"Stop this stupid car!" I punched the dashboard. He pulled over to the curb and started laughing. I looked at him with pity, "You are fucked up,"

He yelled, "And you? Mr. Fucking righteousness!"

I was furious. I retorted, "It's like I am on a road trip with a freaking asshole who doesn't care for anything, and who is trying to push my buttons constantly. I don't want to put up with your constant stupid ass jokes all the time." I got out of the car furiously and put my fists up. "Come on, let's go outside, and see who has got more balls, you or me you asshole!" I wanted to fight him and I didn't care about anything anymore. He wouldn't get out of the car. He just sat and laughed, so I yelled, "What the hell? Come on you think it's funny, well let's see!"

He wouldn't get out of the car, he was just laughing and saying, "Oohhh look at him. He is upset!" He was a real dickhead.

I said fuck it. I went to the back of the car and started collecting my stuff.

He got out of the car and walked up to me, "Oh come on Dimon, where are you going?"

"Home," I Replied.

"Come on man take it easy!" – he said in a more serious voice.

He continued, "Sorry man, I didn't mean it like that, it's just that you ask too many stupid questions. I don't know what I am going to be doing the next minute. You sound just like my wife. I like to cruise man. It gets annoying. Money is just a means to get you from point A to point B. You gotta learn how to just cruise and not get so focused on what are going to eat and where are we going to live. Look around you; you are alive. Stop getting so offended all the time."

I stopped what I was doing and took a breath. "I am not like you. I can't just go on and not worry about not having something to eat," I said.

I turned around and sat on the edge of the trunk. I stared at the far distance and although I was still pissed I realized that's the decisive moment, the one when you make a choice. Either you are going to try to hold on to security or you're going to just allow things to happen to you. After all, that's what I came for: to find a sense of freedom, and here it was, right in front of me, and I was still securing the next moment afraid to experience the present. A voice in my head said "the more you can focus on the present moment the more you defy the rules by which this society lives by, where the primary basic instinct is to attain security."

"What do you want me to do?" he asked and then continued, "All I got is me, myself and I and what I can do with it. My wife never understood that." I retorted, "Fuck You. You are still a dick."

Roman went back to his normal joking self. I got in the car and we started driving. We both switched back to the road, and relished our bi-polarity with The Cure still blasting and this asshole whistling along.

After a while, I said, "I didn't know you had a wife."
He said, "Got a kid too, but whatever man it doesn't matter anymore. I am here now," - and he continued in his normal careless Roman way, "Hey, hey, hey check it out, isn't that an MTV sign over that club. Let's go check it out. The night is young, Romeo."

I shrugged my shoulders and exited the car. At this point in my life, the word "wife and a kid" seemed like a distant island in the middle of the ocean.

Crazy Russians at the MTV Club

I looked to the left and there was a really huge parking lot, and the huge sign read *Panama City Oceanfront Beach Club* and then below that: *Location of the MTV's Spring Break.*

I had seen the live footage of MTV Spring Break on TV before and it always looked tacky, with Jersey Shore techno idiots dancing. Hey, what have we got to lose? We parked our car, put on some shorts and t-shirts, and went inside the club.

The first thing we noticed was a huge pool in the middle of the club. Hip – hop music was blasting; machos in trunks and bimbos in bikinis were mingling to the low bass thumping in the background. It was still early so everyone was just sipping on their drinks in their own little universes. On the right side of the pool there was a big DJ Booth. On top of the booth, hanging over everyone was a beloved MTV sign. To Roman and I, two hippie punks on the road, the place was full of cheap gloss, since the true MTV spirit was long gone from those 3 letters.

Nevertheless, that realization didn't put a damper on our mood, and we went straight to the bar to get warmed up. We got few whiskeys and cokes and went to the beach chairs and extended our feet. After the first few gulps of Jack and Cokes, we were in a much better disposition. People seemed nicer; we were smiling at nobody in particular while one hip – hop song switched to the next. I think this one was "Big Pimpin" by Jay – Z. The whole place had a kind of tropical feel to it: palm trees, surf boards on the walls, stands with shark heads, and girls with Hawaiian flower arrangements around their necks serving drinks.

Some blonde in a bikini came up to us and said, "Hey Guys! How are you? Welcome to Panama City Ocean Beach Club."

Roman looked at her and answered, "Pretty good baby and you?"

She threw us a sparkling glossy smile and came up to Roman, looking over his muscular arms. "I am good. Hey boys, we are holding a Hot Body Contest in few hours, and we want you to be part of it."

I looked at Roman and thought; yeah I could see why they would choose *him*. The guy used to be a professional mountain climber and had an athletic build to hang off of a rock - but why me? I didn't see myself having an athletic build at all, but I figured they asked us both since we were buddies.

I still expressed my doubts and asked, "Are you sure you want me to be part of it as well?"

She smiled and said, "Yeah, both of you guys."

She continued, "DJ will announce your names and you will go over there," – and she pointed at the long walkway with a half circle at the end in the middle of the pool.

We answered, "Sure, what have we got to lose?" We all laughed.

She flushed us her pearly whites again and started to walk away hips swaying, but then she remembered something and returned, "Oh yeah! If you guys have a song you want a DJ to play when you go up there, just give him a CD and he'll play it. See you boys on the runway," – and she walked away to the other group of guys.

I said to Roman, "What do you know? I didn't know we have hot bodies! Ha ha."

He was pulling on his mustache and then smiled mischievously, "We should dazzle them with our grandma skirts and perform Yablochko for them." He laughed loud and evil. "They will all fall off their chairs. Ha ha ha!" I agreed. (Yablochko – an old Russian folk song, traditionally presented as sailors dance)

We decided to dance our version of Yablochko and to show this MTV club something they haven't seen before. We finished our drinks ran to the car and put on our gramma skirts. I found a Russian striped sailor shirt; meanwhile Roman found a matching sailor tank top. As for music, our selection was undoubtedly Gogol Bordello's CD *Voi – La Intruder*. We ran back to the club gave our CD to the DJ, told him what song to put on, got another round of drinks and started to get ready.

I felt wild anticipation for what was about to unfold. The announcement came through the speakers that the hot body contest had begun. At the end of the runway there were about six girls sitting in the half-circle: three on the left side and three on the right. From there the whole club could see you. DJ would announce the names of the contestants and muscle dummies had to walk down that runway, flexing and showing off their steroid pumped muscles, while the girls went screeching like adolescent teenagers.

We stood there making fun of them and had few vodka shots for the success of our legendary performance. To do something like that you needed some vodka shots in advance. All of a sudden, the DJ's voice came through the speakers, "… and now for your pleasure we present Roman and Dmitry from Russia with Love!" That was our cue, "Showtime!"

The song started with Stalin's voice proclaiming in Russian that the duty of every political elector was to be like the great writer, Gogol. (Stalin – a leader of Soviet Union from 1920's to 1953. Was considered the most ruthless Russian dictator that killed more people in concentration camps in Russia than died fighting World War 2. Gogol – great Russian novelist) The intro chords on the guitar and an accordion of the Gogol Bordello song called, "Green card Husband" ripped through the speakers, followed with Eugene Hutz immigrant voice:

And so I married a Chinese lesbian
She was 45 years old
She needed bad to stay in the country
And I needed bad her dough
So I became her Greencard husband
And she became my ten grand wife
We quickly were and happily married
And now we can't split up

Dressed in skirts, whistling like two mad men we jumped on the runway and started dancing like Russian sailors kicking our feet in front. I wished there was a camera to film those faces when they were expecting some buffed up dudes and instead they got two mad Russians dancing around in skirts to gypsy punk. As we were making our way to the end of the runway there were about six girls sitting in half circle that were supposed to praise the contestants. When they saw us they weren't sure how to react, whether to laugh or to run.

When we got close to them we orchestrated a move: we lifted the bottoms of our skirts, and pulled them over the heads of the closest girl sitting below us. The crowd went wild for that. Those people saw something they don't see everyday, and we were ecstatic about being the outcasts. When the music started quieting down we finished our spectacular performance by jumping in the pool. That whole performance lasted for about one minute, but it felt like a lifetime. They were screaming, yelling "Yeaaaaaaah! You Crazy Russians!" Of course, what else can you call Russians?

We got out of the water, somebody was saying we weren't supposed to jump in the water, but we were beyond caring. My memory is fuzzy, but apparently we got a second spot in that contest. We were immigrant rock stars for that moment! People were congratulating us. Everyone wanted to buy a drink for us, and oversized Florida girls were making eyes at us. This chaos went on for few hours, and then things started to get messy. By midnight, we were two drunken sailors barking at each other. We must have had about 15 beers each that night, and our brains were getting messy. Finally I stood there and looked around in drunk stupor and the hip-hop started getting to me so I yelled pointing fingers at everyone, "You are all losers who listen to bad music!" No one could hear me they were too busy bumping even Roman. He was dancing with a fat girl right next to me jiggling her sides and big bosom. I hiccuped then mumbled something that resembled, "Dude I am going to go the beach." I walked towards the ocean. I wanted to go for a swim.

Defending the Liberty of European Swimming Trunks

As I was walking towards the water I noticed a group of wobbling rednecks also going to the water. Roman stayed behind dancing with a fat girl. As I got closer to the beach, one of them approached me. He looked pretty drunk holding on to his Coors light tall can of beer. He stopped to look at me and in his thick southern accent he said laughingly, "Hey commie, those are some gaaaay shorts you are wearing," – and he proceeded laughing and slapping his thighs.

I looked down at my shorts in my drunken stupor. I was wearing European style swim trunks; not exactly Speedos, but regular swim shorts like everyone in Moscow wore to the river. Nothing was wrong with that, I thought. I looked at him and he was wearing those long swim shorts down to his knees and I said, "Well at least they don't look like your swim shorts with shit in them!" –and I laughed really loud, purposely mocking him and pointing a finger. He didn't like that.

"You make fun of me. I am gonna beat your ass down. You wanna fight?" in his slurry speech. His few friends started surrounding us. Roman was nowhere in sight. The redneck walked up to me.

I replied in drunken voice, "Yeah, you are disrespecting my shorts man," and I hiccupped. He was staring me down and I was studying his thick face, blonde short buzz cut hair, blood shot eyes and an extra chin. We were about the same height although he was heavier set. We were breathing alcohol at each other's face. I got an idea.

I started mocking him with an exaggerated Russian accent, "Let's fight a Russ-ssian roulette style, you hit, I hit. You fall, you loooooser. I fall, I lose. Ok?" I wasn't sure if that was Russian style or not, but that seemed like a fun idea.

"Are you reeeeeeeady?" I yelled and hiccupped. "Only one rule! You go first, but you must punch only once," - he nodded back in agreement. His friends yelled and encouraged him, "Come on John! Show this commie!" I yelled, "Davai blya! Do It!" (Davai Blya – Let's go Bitch)

I got ready for a hit, and he took a swing and missed, but then he continued and hit me in my ear and my head a few more times, before I realized this son-of-a-bitch was breaking the rules. I didn't like anyone breaking rules especially when I let him go first.

My ear was ringing and I got angry as if he offended my family's honor and growled back at him. I avoided the last few by taking a step back and I yelled back at him, "You are breaking the rules. I go now!" I continued in Russian, "Suka! Ti ne po pravilam igraesh. Ia tebe pokazhu!" (You bitch, you are not playing by the rules. I will teach you a lesson.)

The angst from hours before was waking up inside me. I advanced on him landing punches in his face and his jaw. Four years of karate and two years of judo started working their way in. He wasn't expecting so many punches falling on him like a wall. I kept shouting, "You broke the rules *Suka*!" I was imagining I was actually fighting Roman and his stupid way of being so carefree and easy going and not giving a fuck. I was crashing all those emotions onto the redneck's face. By some unknown impulse, my right leg went up in the Maya Geri (side kick) and then followed by a front kick. His friends got quiet. I saw blood on his face. I followed him, hitting him over and over senselessly. He started half running away, half backing away. I finally stopped, walked back and looked around for Roman wanting him to witness my victory. All of a sudden he appeared.

I yelled at him energized and victorious, "Dude what the hell? Where were you? Did you see that?"

He answered back, "Relax, I saw it all, I was right there!" He was full of shit. He continued, "I warned you though fighting is not necessary!"

128

I was righteous, I didn't care, "Dude, He didn't like my swim shorts. He was asking for it, plus he broke the rules of our game. He deserved it." I was fighting for the justice and liberty of my European swim trunks. He knew arguing with me was useless, so he laughed and said, "*Horosho, Molodetz poslednii geroi.*" (Good, you are the last hero.)

We saw some dudes from the club running towards us. I had already calmed down and was sobering up. One of them with a sporty build asked us, "Was someone here doing karate kicks?" Looking at us pumped up and ready to show off his moves.

We looked around, shrugged our shoulders and told him, "We don't know man, what you talking about – maybe those guys over there!" We pointed at a group of rednecks leaving towards their hotel, one of which was my opponent wearing long swim trunks. Roman and I tried to hide our smiles. The guys ran in the direction we had pointed.

I was tired but I was feeling victorious. We headed back towards the parking lot and as soon as I got in the car I closed the door and shut my eyes. The thumps from the bass of the club speakers could still be heard faintly in the background like a fucked up digital lullaby.

Why Be Normal?

I woke up as the sun sliced through my eyelids. "Wow, what a fierce sun? Ouch, what a fierce pain!" I felt pain in my right hand. I looked at it and I was shocked by its size. It was the size of a big blue balloon. It was swollen; I could still move my fingers but the palm and the back of my hand had turned blue. I had never experienced anything like that in my life. I woke Roman up, and he looked at me then at my hand as if I was showing him a boring photo.

He yawned and said, "Wow that's big. I didn't know you could make a balloon out of your hand." He smirked and continued, "Hey, you are the one who wanted to fight that guy." I answered a bit scared, "Dude, what do you think is wrong with my hand?" I held it out in front of my face as if it was a new organ of my body that I have never seen before.

He looked at it and said, "I don't know. Maybe you twisted it the wrong way."

I replied worried, "Come on dude, do you think it's broken?"

He looked at me and said, "You wouldn't be able to move your fingers at all if it was broken. Maybe your wrist is sprained. It will take few days to get better that's all," that calmed me down. Maybe he was right, maybe it was just a sprain, I thought.

I remembered last night's fight and felt victorious anyways. I defended the European swimming trunks' honor! I laughed and looked at the sun, the blue sky ahead listening to the sound of the waves that came from the ocean. I romanticized the situation to make myself feel better. I was in Florida, on the road trip and having the time of my life. The fight last night and the blue palm of my hand were just part of being on the road. I fell asleep again. I woke up because Roman closed the car door really loud. He was looking for something in the car. He came back with some duct tape and long pieces of yellow rubber.

I asked him, "What are you going to do with that duct tape?"

He answered smiling, "Wrap your balloon! Ha ha!"

I wasn't laughing. We had no other kind of medical aid so I agreed. He wrapped my hand with yellow pieces of rubber and then taped it around a few more times around. I was content with that.

We decided to get something to eat and I saw a deli across from the parking lot. I went in and grabbed us some sandwiches. My hand was starting to hurt a lot; it was difficult to carry even a little bag with sandwiches. After we ate and inspected my arm one more time I decided that maybe I should go to the emergency room.

I said to him, "Dude, I think I got to go and check it out, I am not sure if it's broken, but it's getting big." He looked at me and agreed that maybe it was the right thing to do. We packed our stuff in the car and drove looking for the hospital.

We looked like two hobos in skirts. We felt dirty, unshaven, and out of place. In the emergency room, though, the ladies didn't mind our looks and were seemingly quite entertained. One of them in a crisp white nurse's outfit looked at my arm and asked, "Did you bandage it yourself with this yellow duct tape?" – she was smiling.

I answered proudly, "No, my friend did it!"

As she cut the duct tape off, she said, "It looks like it's broken!" I was trying to fight it, "Maybe it's just swollen, or sprained; maybe it will go away." She looked at me with disapproval and continued, "We are still going to have to take some X-Rays."

After the X-rays, she came back and showed me my hand; I looked at the bones of my hand in the X-Ray and thought is that what the hand really looks like under the skin? We are really skeletons underneath it all. I didn't know where to look for the break and then she showed me a fracture on my palm next to the pinky. She said look and showed me a small piece of my bone sticking out. I agreed with her professional opinion that it was broken and I needed a cast for my hand. I thought, "Damn, how stupid of me."

As I was waiting in the room for the doctor to put my hand in the cast the nurse came back smiling and asked me, "Is that your friend wearing a blue skirt and a green hat in the waiting room?"

I said, "Yeah, why?" She continued, "He asked me to tell you that he is doing well, and that he has made friends with the ladies at the reception room."

"That definitely sounds like my friend," I answered smiling.

After they put my hand in the cast, it covered my arm to the elbow, and the only thing I could see were my fingers sticking out. When I came out Roman was standing on one of the chairs, trying to balance while everyone was laughing. I was happy to see Roman having fun again and being himself. He looked at me and threw at me a line from a Russian movie called, *The Diamond Hand,* "What a beautiful cast, are you by any chance carrying diamonds in there?"

The Diamond Hand

The plot consists of a Russian tourist who, after slipping on a banana peel in a foreign country, loses consciousness. While he remains unconscious, he is picked up by a band of local mobsters who put his arm in a plaster cast with huge diamonds inside to smuggle it back to his country. Of course it happened that they got the wrong guy, otherwise there would have been no movie. To make a long story short, my cast looked very similar to the one from that movie. Roman knocked on my plaster cast, laughed and said, "Let's go jewelry smuggler." I grinned and wiggled my fingers.

We got out of the hospital and walked back to the car. I was relieved that this whole thing was over. He ran to a grocery store to get a pack of cigarettes. When he came back, he pasted this huge red sticker in front of my passenger seat that read, "WHY BE NORMAL?" I laughed long and loud. Yeah, that definitely summed up our experience.

My Parking Lot Theory

After the hospital, we wanted to clean up our act and to try to be responsible for once. It was decided that we would clean our car first since it turned into a complete mess and the only place that was familiar to us was the parking lot in front of that damned Panama City Ocean Beach club where I broke my hand. Also, we decided to go back there and to take apart our little house on wheels since we were sure there would be no parked cars and we could really use the space. While we were cleaning the car, I took a drag from a weed roach we found and developed a whole theory about parking lots that I naturally called, my *Parking Lot Theory*.

Parking lots are the new bars of the 21st century. When we ride in the car, we share our world with those people inside our car, but when we park our mutually shared world externalizes. This is the place where you can run into all kinds of adventures, and your fate chooses the people it brings you. If one decides to interact with them, then that person's life may change, and the destination may be altered and a valuable lesson may be acquired in the process. I scored my first acid from some hippies that were tripping out at the parking lot after the *Doors of the 21st Century* concert. I got kicked out of that concert by the first half of the show to the sounds of Ray Manzarek pounding away on his keys, "Run with me " and six bouncers were escorting me out. I thought, Jimmy Morrison would have been proud of me. The point was that the Doors of Perception are always there; if you are looking to crack them open, a parking lot is as good a place as any.

Trailer Park John

We were parked right in the middle of a huge empty parking lot while the bright Florida sun was shining on us with all of its scorching merciless valor. We opened all the car doors and windows and we were taking it very easy with some music on the background. Roman put on the brightest Woodstock tie-dye shirt, while I sported last night's smelly tee since I had no other clothes and needed to wash them somewhere. It was getting really hot.

Aside from the mess we created, I had no idea there was so much other crap in Roman's car. It looked like our car was a dinosaur that just threw up all over this parking lot. Just to name a few peculiar things that I spotted were: masks, wigs, the axe, a jockey helmet, golf clubs, ladies' underwear, a toy ball, skiing poles, Hawaiian clothes, goggles for flying, a huge video camera, ties, carpenter tools, and of course our axed down flags.

As we were standing there examining everything, I saw some dude walking across the parking lot towards us. By the looks of him he wasn't going to give us a winning lottery ticket or try to sell us a time-share in Florida – to be honest, he looked more like a bum. As he got closer I saw that he was tall and skinny guy with a baseball hat, a dirty jean jacket and ripped up jeans. When he got closer I could see his face and it looked like he had gotten in a bad brawl last night. His face was beat up to a point that his right eye was swollen and blue and his nose was red probably from drinking every night.

Growing up in New York you learn to classify bums according to their appearance within seconds. Junkies, alcoholics, bums, and hobos all pretty much ask for the same thing: change. You learn how to just look the other way and say, "Sorry, I don't have any change," and keep on swimming inside a dirty human sea called the subway, hoping they leave you alone. That attitude usually got you through those situations, but this guy was walking directly towards us and there was no one else around. He had already put a toothless smile on his unshaven face as a greeting. When he started asking us for money I already had an answer ready, but Roman was as happy to see him as if he was an old childhood friend. He asked him what was his name, where was he from and where was he going, and after that shook hands with him. I looked at his hands; they were a workman's hands, bruised from hard labor and street fighting. He told us his name was John something or other. He lived fifteen minutes away from this parking lot and he was just collecting change for the bus to get a ride back home. According to his foul smell he had one too many beers last night and had a pretty similar adventure to mine. We were young, and those nights were expected. In his case, it was more of a lifestyle.

Roman and John hit it off famously like old pals. I almost felt that Roman did that on purpose to piss me off. Every time I was acting on a New Yorker impulse Roman was acting on a Californian upbringing, as if trying to show me how jaded I was. Roman started asking him whether he had any family. This guy answered, "Yeah, I got me a wife and a daughter and my ma livin' out back in Alabama".

When Roman heard that John had a family he got really excited – "You got any photos?"

John said yeah, and he reached in his jeans pocket for his wallet, meanwhile Roman ran to the driver's seat to fetch his wallet, as if it was a dire emergency they had to see each other's family photos. I was getting really hungry and wasn't really taking part in their bullshit excitement. I already knew where the sandwich store was so I just told those two buddies that I am going to go and get a sandwich. I went to the store letting them have a good ol' jolly time. The guy at the counter asked me, "Looks like you had yourself some fun last night?"

I smiled back at him, half in amusement and half in regret, and answered, "Yeah I came out a winner from a beach kickboxing championship." The guy from the deli gave me a quick smirk seeing I was not in the mood to discuss this matter any further. When I was walking back, I really hoped the guy would have split by now, but from far away I saw that they were still standing there laughing. I couldn't believe it, both of them acting as if they were buddies.

Roman was able to find his way into the hearts of people no matter who they were. He made friends with few words, knowing what to say and what face to put on. He fed off of people, he entertained them, he was their hero, he made their senseless lives fun for a moment. For some reason he found alliance with those down on their luck. He more than empathized, he encouraged them that it was OK to be who they were, to be down on their luck, to be in need or in pain. Somehow I felt it was just a cover up. I didn't know the details of Roman's life yet, but I knew there would be a moment when I would find out what he was running from. He was having a time of his life on the surface, but he closed off the source of his issues and he wasn't going to let anyone make him weaker.

I sat on the asphalt next to the car and I started eating. I noticed John's hungry stare at my sandwich. I sighed and gave him a half and Roman did the same with his. Roman announced that John could score us a twenty bag of weed if we drive him back to his home. I asked where was that, and John said looking at me not trusting me enough completely, "It's at the trailer park down the road about fifteen minutes from here." I grumbled to myself, "Yeah that meant a free ride for him," he was staring at me with those innocent blue eyes one would have thought he was still in kindergarten asking his teacher if he can go play outside.

After we ate Roman finished cleaning his car and it was unbelievable. I exclaimed, "Holy Shit! I can't believe this piece of shit could look so nice and have so much space." We all got in and went to

John's house. John grinned with his toothless smile; I think the bastard was pretty happy to have made some new friends and to be given a ride. I started noticing John's boyish look about him and how he must have been a young boy once, full of wild dreams and how meeting us must have triggered the feeling of being young again, since now he was laughing at our stupid jokes.

We were driving down one of those smooth Floridian local two way roads with huge trees hanging over the highway when John leaned over to Roman and said, "Buddy, hang a neeeext leeeeft, right there?" He pointed to one of those little dirt roads that led to a little opening between the trees. Roman took a left and slowly drove in savoring every moment as if he was entering through the gates of Rome. There it was, John's trailer park.

It was an open area with trees all around with old trailers parked in half circle. On the right, there was a group of local trailer park citizens sitting on the porch of one of the trailers, drinking beers and smoking cigarettes. On the left, there was a lonely pickup truck without wheels. The trunk of that pickup truck was full of empty beer cans forming a pyramid. There were many empty cans scattered all around it on the ground.

When we rode in, the men were laughing loudly, but as soon as we parked our car and got out, they stopped laughing and it turned quiet all of a sudden. They were looking at John and at us, curious to know our purpose there - we obviously didn't look like we belonged. It was awkward. Roman was ecstatic, and he was taking it all in. He looked as if he stepped into a museum of modern art. He noticed my round eyes and jerked his head back with his upper lip curled.

When we walked up to them closer, their physical appearance resembled their lifestyles. They all had round bellies and their faces were red from alcohol and the sun. John asked them in his southern accent, "Those boys are nice. They are drivin' out west and gave me a lift up here. They wanna know if we got 'em any green smokes left?"

They relaxed a bit and one of them said, "Hey, how's it goin' boys?"

The guy in a baseball hat, a dirty wife beater and the big beard of a Harley rider spoke to John slowly, "Hey Johnny, go check my trailer, you know where."

John turned to us and said, "You boys hang out here, I'm gonna go and check his trailer," - and he walked off towards the trailer in the distance. He left us standing there just looking around. It was awkward.

I wiped the sweat off my face. It was getting very hot. We found out that the burly guy's name with a big beard was Steve. He asked us, "You boys want a beer?"

Roman looked at me and said, "Yeah sure." The guy gave us two tall blue cans of Coors Light.

I saw sweat dripping off my nose and should have said no and asked for some water instead, but I thought Coors Light was just as good as water so it will be fine. Roman already started talking to one of the guys about living in Florida. I looked towards the direction John went and saw him coming back. I hoped he had good news, since I just wanted to get the hell out of this trailer park and go for a swim.

John came back looked at Roman with a sorry face and said, "Sorry we are all out. We had few bags left yesterday, but we smoked them all," and he graced us with a toothless smile. Roman told him it's ok not to worry about it and continued talking to one of the guys.

The Toothless Queen of the Trailer Park

I felt uncomfortable. I motioned to Roman to start leaving, but he didn't seem like he wanted to go. All of a sudden, out of the trailer park behind the group of drinking men walks out this short skinny woman with long blonde hair, jean shorts and a t-shirt. She looked as thin as a stick, and when she turned to face us, maaaan I thought I saw one ugly witch, a sister of *Baba Yaga. Baba Yaga* is a fairy tale witch character in Russian literature with long grey hair, missing teeth, and a broom for transportation, which she used for creating mischief everywhere. That's what that woman looked like. That scariest thing was that out of the thirty-six teeth she must have had only six left.

She was in a good mood until she saw John and started hissing at him, "You old dog tried to grab me real hard last night. It's a good thing Ron gave you a beating." Steve handed her a beer and she started gulping the beer down, drinking it non-stop and when she was done she threw that can at the back of that pickup truck. The can didn't make it in the trunk and stayed lying on the ground as an artifact of a lifestyle.

John was getting heated up, "You old hag. Mind your own business you heaaar. It wasn't like that. If you had any brains you would stay outta my business!"

I wanted to get out of there badly. Suddenly, she noticed us and turned around to study Roman and I. Her eyes were glistening; she was smiling with her 6 teeth and her face looked ugly, real ugly. Admiring Roman's strong arms she started hitting on him. She started speaking and whistling through s's and h's and spitting through the b's. "What a BOOOY! He's shhhoo cayute!"

The group of men started laughing. Steve told her, "Marge! Let 'em be, the boys just travelin' west to California," but she was unstoppable.

She came up to him and started poking at his arms and showering us with her toothless smiles and alcoholic breath. Roman was not an amateur with the ladies so he responded to such advances with a musketeer smile.

142

All of a sudden, he runs to the car. She yelled, "Where do you think you going?"

He pressed play on our Gogol Bordello cd, grabbed that scary witch and yelled, "Lady, you wanna dance?"

She was waiting all her life for that question. She yelled, "You bettcha I do!"

He grabbed her and they started dancing away in the middle of the trailer park to the lyrics of our all time favorite song: *I got a Passport Officer*. I was standing next to the passenger's door and I started laughing.

Those drunken men were all in tears; they were ecstatic, "Yeah! Come on Marge! Dance you old hag! Show that boy your moves." Roman and Marge were twirling to the music. That was the time of that's lady's life; she was cackling like the toothless drunken witch that she was.

They were twirling around and around; all of a sudden I realized I was falling. I only had enough time to grab hold of the car's door. I looked at Roman asking him to help. He saw me falling, ran to hold me up and told me to hold on to the door. Meanwhile he dug out a gallon of emergency water we had somewhere in the trunk and screamed at me, "Drink!" I drank the warm water and started to feel a little better immediately. I felt the water filling up every pore of my body. I hadn't had any water since my trip to the hospital.

Roman looked at me and said, "Dimon, you are having a sunstroke. You gotta take a cold shower quick!"

143

My eyes were half open, everything was moving, I felt half alive and mumbled, "But where? We don't' have a hotel room?"

He said, "Here in one of the trailers, there has got to be a shower." He turned around to John and asked, "You got a shower in your trailer, right?"

John answered, "Yeah."

Roman continued, "Can you let him use it real quick? He is having a sunstroke!"

John said, "Sure. Whatever you need."

I looked in the direction of his trailer and my mind was fighting it, but the necessity spoke for itself. As Roman walked me towards his trailer, John yelled, "Just turn left for cold and right for hot."

I got into the shower, turned on the cold water and sat on the floor of the bathtub hugging my knees. The cold stream was hitting my head I closed my eyes and exhaled. I felt much better. I didn't realize that sun is not a joke and you can pass out if you are not drinking water. I stayed there for about 10 minutes. As I shut off the water I stood there thinking that people are people wherever you go. No matter if they live in the slums, trailer parks, or their cars, they will come and help you if you treat them like people. I got out of the shower and looked around the room. Aside from being messy, there was nothing unusual about it: a bed, a little table, old dirty lamp and magazines on the floor. I realized there is no "us and them." We are all just trying to live life in our own ways.

I walked up to John and said, "Thank you so much John. I don't know what I would have done without that shower."

He looked pleased and gave me a boyish grin, "Hey you better put your hat on, ya know in this heat."

I smiled back and answered, "Yeah I will."

The fun was over and the toothless lady went back inside the house as the men shared a cigarette. The trailer park didn't look so menacing anymore but it was just a home to those people like any other. They might not have luxuries and too many choices, but maybe it's better this way. Simpler. Well...maybe not for your liver. I smirked at my own thoughts.

Roman looked at me with approval and said, "Are we ready to go now?"

I answered, "Yeah let's go."

As we got in the car, John ran up to us, and asked, "Hey, can ya gimme a lift back to town?"

I answered, "Sure. No Problems." Roman nodded and we put on a new CD, and drove out of the trailer park.

John in the Flying Car

When we got back to town Roman suddenly got serious. He squinted and was pulling on his mustache in silence. I knew something was up I asked, "What's up?"

"Shit Man. We got to change our transmission fluid, the engine light is on and we can't drive without it for too long."

I asked, "Well how much is that?"

Roman said, "I don't know. Around 40…45 bucks!"

I didn't like that answer, "Fuck, we are going to be broke again. Do we need it pretty bad?"

Roman replied, "Yep, unless you want to fly without the engine."

We decided to take care of it instantly. We spotted a body shop and pulled in. As we got out of the car we noticed John snoring in the back seat. We tried everything to wake him up: moving him from side to side, yelling in his ear, "John, wake Up! Time to go to school!" John was snoring right though all our attempts. The mechanic was getting impatient, since he had other cars pulling in, so we told him just leave the snoring specimen in the car. Apparently the rowdy night finally took his toll on him. The mechanic nodded with a smile and added, "Just lock the doors so he won't jump out if he wakes up all of sudden." We locked all the doors, but left the windows open.

We stood there watching the mechanic raise the car almost to the ceiling. John immediately woke up and started yelling, "Where am I? Why is this car taking off? I don't want to go. Let me out of here!" The poor bastard thought he was going to meet his maker.

We laughed because that's exactly what we wanted to hear. We yelled at him to stop moving, "No John don't get out! We were trying to wake you up, but you wouldn't move man, so just keep sleeping." He realized he had no way out, so he went back to sleep, and we went to have some Chinese food at the local restaurant across the street.

When we came back our car was fixed, it was parked next to the car shop. John was awake and a bit sore about us leaving him in the car. He kept repeating, "I can't believe you boys left me up in there. I wake up, and me thinks I got abducted man!" We drove him to the bus stop, where he wanted to go initially that morning. I told him it was time for us to go, and he got kind of sentimental. He even said, "You boys made my life a good ol' time today. Have a safe trip to the West Coast now ya hear." We were touched; we both took turns hugging him. This time I didn't really care that his eye was swollen and his clothes were dirty. The man helped me out and that's what's important.

Stealing Gas for The Road out of Florida

The sun was setting and the luscious trees were hanging by the sides of the highway, it was dusk and we were on the road again. I felt drenched with all the events that occurred in the past few days, as we drove further into the heart of America. As we were driving out of Florida, the troubles weren't ready to let us go just yet. We wanted to get some food, and I had to face an unwanted truth. We were broke again. When I tried to take out money at the ATM, there was this unnerving minus sign before the balance of my account, which added a certain twitch to my face. I went negative in my bank account without a way to save it. Not that it bothered me, but reality was knocking on our door again, and I hated reality. I was getting annoyed. I didn't want to deal with it. We spent all the money my mother wired me. The question was where are we going to get money again? The gas in the car was running low.

While we munched on a grilled sandwich purchased by the coins we collected from the car, I suddenly got an idea. As we were pondering on that idea, that idea grew horns, and a tail and a little red figure with crooked teeth started dancing on my left shoulder and cracking up louder and louder with it's evil laughter. It kept repeating, "Do something illegal! Bwa – ha – ha – ha! Steeeeeeeeeeeeeal!"

Yep that's right, having no other options but to keep moving, we decided to steal some fuel from the gas station. We didn't know how to do it yet, but we wanted to try it. We pulled into some random gas stations and observed how people paid for gas. The new way of paying for gas in most cases was for people to get out of their cars and swipe their credit card, but some gas stations were still old fashioned. You had to go to the cashier and give them your credit card or cash, then you had to go and fill up your car and when you were done, you had to go back to the booth again and sign the receipt. That's what we were looking for. Roman takes out a bunch of credit cards from his glove compartment, makes a fan out of them and starts fanning himself imitating a proper 19th century lady, "Eenie- mini – miny – mo catch a redneck by the toe, who is the lucky bastard whose card we are going to use today to buy some gas with?"

I looked at him with a big question mark in my pupils, he replied calmly as usual, "Don't worry they are all expired!"

My worried pupils turned into big red pupils and I growled with a voice other than my own, "Fuck it, let's do it, amigo!"

We stopped at this desolate and lonely gas station illuminated only by the light of the street lamps. There were a few cars filling up and it was one of those "pay the cashier" types of gas stations. Roman turned to me and said, "While I go and give them this credit card, you have to start filling it up. Here is a black marker, go to the license plate and make a 3 into a 9 and 6 into an 8." I looked at him and I saw on his left shoulder a red-horned wicked little monster doing hula-hoops.

I knew that it was risky, because with the license they could just track down the car, and car owner, and things would be over pretty soon, but that's why this genius of mischief actually had a good idea. But what's a road trip without some rock-n-roll? While Roman went to pay for gas with his fake credit card on someone else's name, I started pumping gas. I noticed Roman making small talk with the ladies, as he always was. While the gas was pumping, I went to the back of the car, kneeled down by the license plate and changed the number 3 into an 8, and 1 into a 7. From far away you couldn't tell what they were. As he was walking back, I nodded to him signaling everything was ready. Agent 007 music went on in my head again and Action!

My heart was pounding. It felt like it was the slowest gas station in the world. It was all a matter of how soon the cashier realized that our credit cards didn't work. Digits were turning slowly on the pump dial. The lady who was processing the credit card from the booth looked at us, and then looked back down. She got up and started moving towards the door, and that was a sure sign it was time to take off. Part II of the plan went into action - The Escape. Roman jumped in the car and floored the gas pedal. I barely made it in after taking the pump out. I jumped in as he floored the gas pedal, and my door was swinging left to right, but Roman made a sharp left turn and the door closed. The gas station was in our rear view mirror and we could see that lady screaming and cursing our name.

She ran back to the cashier booth. The deed was done and we had three-quarters of a tank. We were happy for a moment until it started settling on us, that she could just tell cops that we were driving a green SUV Nissan and what highway we went down. We decided to take the next exit and suddenly saw a cop car standing by the exit. As we passed the police car, the sirens all of sudden turned on and he took off right behind us. Our hearts thumped in our ears, and we signaled to pull over.

Lady Luck was on our side again. As the cop leveled his car with ours, looked inside and saw two scared white boys he chose to pursue a black car in front of us with tinted windows and hip-hop blasting at full volume. We weren't speeding - we were just scared shitless, well at least I was. All the way to Louisiana, I was worrying they would catch up with us, and what would await us if they did. One time, I spent few hours in jail for the most stupid thing in the world: jumping over the turnstile inside the subway just because I wanted to make it to the train. Aside from not making that train, I also cursed out the cop and spent a few hours in the precinct jail. When I got out of that precinct jail, I was breathing in the air of freedom like never before in my life.

We were relieved once we crossed the Louisiana border, free from Florida cops. I sighed deeply and decided that we weren't going to steal any more gas. Once we crossed the border, I went to the first payphone, phoned home to my ever-loving and giving mother, and asked her to wire us some more money for the road trip. My mother, of course, was cross-examining me: how was the trip, and how were we doing? When I told her that I broke my arm, she rained me with the questions of how and why.

After I calmed her down and I asked her for the money she replied, "What happened to the last three hundred dollars I sent you few days ago?" I had to promise that all would be returned when I get back. On that note we drove towards New Orleans - the city of the blues and no sunrises.

New Orleans, Extreme Debauchery!

New Orleans - city of blues, witches, all night partying, even more drinking and very little rules. I'd been dreaming about this city. I had never visited it, but I always wanted to. Now we were driving on the wings of mischief and a belief that everything happens to those who seek. Santana was blasting through the speakers *Got a Black Magic Woman...* Route 10 was ours, and the wind was taking us there faster than we were driving. As we were approaching New Orleans, I managed to get some sleep, since the events of Florida had taken a toll on me. I was mentally exhausted. Finally, when we arrived at the infamous French Quarter of New Orleans, Roman woke me up.

Since the cars weren't allowed to go any further, we decided to change our clothes in the car and leave it parked. My outfit for the night was a white curtain as a skirt, tucked in British flag, golf club as a walking stick, beads - down to my knees, huge "Raver" dark sunglasses, and a hand in a cast. Roman's outfit was a long white Indian shirt, blue skirt with bright blue flowers, red bandana, green hat, small round sunglasses, golf club, and a smile. We were ready for New Orleans. It was midnight, and we were in the middle of it all: crowds of people roaming the streets, drunken laughter, loud men, loose women, neon lights, live music blasting from left and right, strip clubs, bars, advertisements for cheap shots, and even washboard solos. It felt like a carnival, even though there was no specific holiday going on. Here you felt like something ancient woke up inside and wanted out. The throbbing rhythm of life was eager to drown itself in the overindulgence of human senses.

We walked into the first bar with the sign over the door that read *Funky Pirate*. The band was playing right next to the entrance, horns were blowing in our faces, and the guitars were endlessly soloing. It was a big bar with a second floor. In the middle of the bar, there was this pickup truck with little toy dinosaurs glued to the hood of the car, and lights and all kinds of weird stuff. We thought it would be fun to take a picture.

All of a sudden everyone started yelling and clapping. We looked in that direction and saw two women bartenders. One was laying on her back on the bar, while the other one was holding a shot of tequila and licking a line of salt from her stomach nice and slow. Everyone went berserk and started whistling. There were waitresses in mini skirts walking around offering mini-shots in test tubes on a tray. We immediately

153

grabbed a few tubes and Roman made a bet with one of the waitresses that if he could drink his shot with his nose, she should give him another one for free. Of course he couldn't do it, and he ended up coughing and sneezing and everything ended up spilling on his t-shirt. The waitress got kicks out of watching him try, so she gave us two free shots anyway.

Woman created the blues, and in this city the blues ruled man's hearts. Those few chords dictated your feelings, and on top of the simple drum patterns laid the root notes of the blues progressions. The guitars were yelling, screeching, and praising the pleasures of the body and the devastation of the next morning. The blues man, the preacher from down below, was delivering his sermon.

Sue and Gloria

After listening to the band and having a few shots each, we hit the streets to check out another Bourbon Street attraction – a local strip bar. We went to the first strip joint across the street from the Funky Pirate. When we walked inside, the bar was on the right and a few people in the middle were watching the show from the stools here and there. The stage was on the left and some lonely lady was holding on to the pole as she was pulling her bra off. The room was half empty since the night was still at its peak and everyone was polishing off their drinks somewhere else. As the night progressed, one dancer would walk off the stage followed by random claps and whistles, and a new woman would walk up the stairs to perform a decadent snake dance for the mesmerized lizards. We watched those wasted women holding on to the rail. Some of them were overweight. Some were midgets, and some were just really strange and zoned out. We were slowly turning into the lizards ourselves as we were waiting for something to happen.

I noticed someone looking at us. I motioned to Roman to look that way, and there, at the back of the bar, they were two completely decked out, gorgeous girls, or should I say women, wearing little skirts and high heels. They were pointing at us and whispering. We were no fools ourselves, so we started eyeing them back. It was very odd to see those two not dancing on stage, since they would make this place look lively. At the next instance, they got up, and started walking out of the place.

I kicked Roman's shoulder, "Dude, let's go talk to them."

Roman fixed his mustache and exclaimed, "Youngling, when does the bull go to the cow? The bull waits until the cow gives him a sign."

I replied anxiously, "Well they are giving us all kinds of signs."

He said, "Just smile at them, as they are leaving."

We were standing there smiling looking our crooked best. As they were leaving one of them came up to us and smiling a bit with her full red lips, she said, "Nice skirts boys!" and left a note on the bar obviously for us to read. She waved with her fingers in a black laced glove a little good-bye gesture and walked out slowly swaying those hips left to right. A crooked thought, just like a cockroach, crawled up in my mind, "is that real hair?" The smell of her really strong perfume and red lipstick filled my nostrils, and I forgot about that thought real quick. My twenty two year old balls were full to the brim, and my little brother was awake and screaming capriciously at the top of his lungs, "I want that. Follow that."

Our mouths were dry as we read the note, *Boys – meet us across the street at the back of Slinky's.* I turned around to Roman and in his playful eyes a sparkle of mischief was burning strong. He licked his lips and said, "See my impatient youngling, now the bull can proceed down to the valley, because the cows have given him a signal, so we might as well follow the note and find out what is at the back of that Slinky's bar?"

We finished our drinks and went outside. As soon as we walked out across the street we saw the sign, *Slinky's* in bright neon lights, and we went inside. It looked more like a lounge with toned down music and lots of couches everywhere. We went straight to the bar and got two whiskeys. Taking sufficient gulps each for bravity we proceeded to the back. The back was dimly lit, and there were booths with tables here and there. As we went in, we saw them waving at us. My heart was thumping. Roman was pulling on his mustache and licking his lips like a cat ready for a mouse. We came up to them and smiled. They were sipping on the little straws inside their drinks. We sat down, and Roman said, "Ladies, we have to find out the names of such fine works of art."

One of them said, "Sue" and giggled, and the other one followed, "Gloria."

Little did I know back then that those names were not real, but what did I care, my penis answered, "Very nice to meet you."

The conversation turned to silence as we struggled to say something amusing. I was sitting behind the table with Gloria on one couch and Roman was on the other couch with Sue a few feet away. I felt Gloria's hand reaching under my skirt and slide up my leg. My leg was on fire. I looked at Roman. He was hugging Sue. He was necking with her in between sips on his cocktail. Meanwhile, Gloria got closer to my ear, licked it, and whispered in a lower tone than usual, "I would like to find out what's underneath this skirt of yours!" I felt like I needed some water.

I turned to her and said, "I don't know, there are people." She slowly started sliding under the table, and put her finger on her red lips in a hush sign. I felt my skirt going up and I was about to burst. I looked around. There were few couples on the far end of the room, but apparently they were too into each other to care what was going on around them. Her mouth closed against my skin. Her lips were moist and I moaned. I've had blowjobs before but nothing like this. I couldn't last long. It was too good. I was ready to come when I heard Roman yell in Russian, "Blya oni muzhiki" which in English meant, "Fuck, they are men!"

I had my eyes closed, but when I realized what that phrase meant, I felt as if ice water was splashed in my face. I jumped up from my seat as if I got burned. I was yelling, "Ahhhhh!"

Roman jumped up on the bench, "Blya, he, she! U nee chlen k noge priviazan! (His penis is tied to her leg!)"

157

I retorted, "Poshli otsuda. (Let's go.)" They were looking at us with innocent eyes, like they didn't know what was going on.

Sue said in a deep man's voice, "Leaving so fast boys?" licking his lips sprawled on the couch like a sphinx. We ran outside.

Johnny's Locksmith Blues

We kept running until we got out of the Bourbon street club zone, only returning to a walking pace once far away. We saw another bar in a completely desolate neighborhood called "Blacksmith Joint," and we walked in. There was a nice, dim and relaxed vibe in there, and we could hear a piano playing at the back. It was some old guy singing, "Do you know what it means to miss New Orleans." Roman went straight to the bathroom to wash his hands. When he came back I went to the bathroom to wash everything else, but I still felt his mouth wrapped around my penis. We got another beer. At first I was just chuckling, then smiling, then I couldn't hold it, "Were we just trying to make it with two hot looking dudes? Ha ha ha!"

Roman was wiping his hands on his t-shirt. He said, "Man, I was making out with her, and then I put my hand on her ass, and then I went to the front, and I felt that thing tied to his leg!" He kept going, "and you know what the craziest thing was? Was that she had real boobs that makes her a he-she. I guess a she-male." I was laughing long and loud. He was getting upset, "What about you? You were getting sucked off, and you were enjoying it a little too much!"

I replied, "Yeah you are right! It was so good I couldn't even tell the difference. Although, I couldn't tell if the hair was real or not." We were sipping on beers and laughing. I said, "This is probably the best story yet from the whole road trip."

The sounds of the piano started picking up and we moved to the back room where the piano player was barely visible from behind his piano. He was old, but his enthusiasm was far exceeding his age. The room wasn't that big. It had tables here and there with candles. It was a real New Orleans type of scenario. We found out the piano player's name was Johnny. Every time he paused between the songs, he would whip out this toy that looked like a crocodile that snapped its jaws. He could manipulate opening and closing of the toy crocodile's mouth. He went around the piano repeating, "Feed the Crocky, Feed the Crocky. Put some money in the Crocky," while the toy crocodile's jaw was snapping. That was very funny. We kept feeding the Crocky with dollar bills, so Johnny turned to us, "Where are you fellas from?"

We answered, "We are driving from New York, going to California!"

He continued, "I hear a bit of an accent, where is the accent from?"

We answered, "from Russia."

He said, "Ah I knew it!" I got a perfect song for you and he started pounding an old famous song about Moscow evenings that even my parents used to sing. It made us feel good because he sped it up twice as fast and turned it into tango rhythm towards the end of it. It was a lot of fun to hear this guy from New Orleans play a familiar tune in a whole new way. We were happy so we get more drinks that cost us only few bucks. That's the best thing about New Orleans you can get completely trashed on 10 dollars. This time we went for something heavier. Jack with Coke was my drink. When we get back, Johnny was taking a pause. As he was musing on the next song, he turned to the right, and said something towards the darkness at the back of the room, "Hey Marge, lay off the fella, come and sing a tune with me?" I looked in the direction Johnny was talking towards and saw there was this couple making out. It was very dark in that corner so they were using it to their own advantage.

When Marge heard her name, she unglued herself from her partner, slowly stood up, fixed her hat, turned around and started making her way to the piano without saying a single word. She was tall, good-looking with dark hair. She was wearing an old hat from the twenties, a black blouse, jeans, and black boots. Apparently she already had a few drinks. She was wobbly, but she had everyone's attention. We were watching her every move. She grabbed the microphone leaned against the wall, lit up a cigarette and said in a raspy voice, "All right Johnny play my song." It was a mesmerizing moment, and we forgot about the events that took place before we got to this bar. In this bar, time stopped completely. Johnny started playing this tune that everyone knew. The lyrics went like this:

Come over, spend a little time with me sometime
Boy, you'd better let me know that you still want to be mine
You know it doesn't cost that much
We really ought to stay in touch
So come over, baby come over
& spend a little time with me sometime

This girl had a deep and raspy voice. She was almost half whispering, half singing. The song was amazing, because they slowed down the tune, allowing her to sing in the spaces more. It was as if she was the seduction, and we were the strangers. We were listening to her every word. When the song died down no one was clapping; everyone was mesmerized, because her last words "… with me sometime" were still in the air.

Johnny said, "Margaret everyone! Put your hands together for our lovely Margaret!" Everyone clapped, and the Crocky's jaws of course went snapping for some cash. She put the microphone down and walked back to the corner where the lustful young partner was watching her from the dark corner of his, waiting to get his fill of her seductive essence. His embrace was twice as strong now that she shared herself with all of us in the room. Meanwhile Johnny was onto the next song. We sang a few more songs with Johnny that night, and then we ventured back out into the streets. We took a different route and walked toward the river.

In the dark alleys, the lucky ones that scored in the basics of street conversation were now moving further into the private worlds of strangers they just met. Hands were sliding under the skirts; hungry lips with smeared lipstick caressed the phallus. As the night progressed, it seemed like the streets were raping the morals. The bedrooms were shaking, and orgasms were drowned out by the cry for more. In the mornings, half of them would be regretting what they had done, and they would go out on the streets, hear those bluesmen tell their age-old tales. Bluesmen would praise their love for sins and play those ancient and familiar few chords and the hearts of their listeners would rejoice from the spells of their melodies. The people listening would contemplate their lives, and then they would ask for another drink while the clock on the wall was counting down toward the ultimate abyss: the next morning.

Revelations from the Mississippi River

The night was warm, and after a few blocks, we ended up walking right into the Mississippi river. We had fresh beers in our hands, and we were laughing about something stupid. From far away we could see the ships in the distance, more like the replicas of turn of the century steamboats with their lights on. Some homeless musician was blowing on the sax quietly, and the river was flowing on its course toward the sea. I looked at that flowing water and thought for a moment. I am on this trip because I said yes to life. Up to this point so many things happened that I wasn't able yet to understand, but it was happening to me, and all around me. When one is physically moving through space, the eyes and the body are experiencing changes. The eyes are seeing things and the body is moving through the air, and yet the mind needed some time to catch up.

I realized that I had never been so free in my life. My possessions and my attachments were few, and I had no one to tell me what to do. I was the king of my own life. The fact that I found myself in this city was proof that I was on the journey, unfolding its endless possibilities for us over and over again. We make a turn here: one set of adventures awaits us. We make a turn there, and a different set of adventures awaits. You might never see the people you meet again, but the fact that you see another life in front of you is a living manifestation that they are also on their own road trip- the road trip called life.

Roman asked, "Dimon u ok?"

I said, "Yeah man, I was just thinking about something." - and then my phone rang. I was getting a phone call from Queens from my roomate Vlad. He quickly and rapidly started telling me something. I couldn't understand him right away. He spoke like a stuttering machine gun. I told him to slow down so I could understand. He wanted me to beware of Roman, that he was a thief and a liar, and that he had stolen a video camera from his friends at the K.S.P. festival in the woods where

163

they met. I should call the cops and tell on him immediately.

I remembered that there was a camera in the car with no case for it - and I looked at Roman. Roman didn't know what Vlad was telling me, but he guessed and was yelling, "Vlad, I love you too!" I told Vlad to calm down and that I would call him later. He was still talking when I hung up. I thought to myself that Roman probably had stolen that camera, but somehow I didn't really care what he stole or from whom. I knew he would probably sell the camera and he will put the money in his pocket. I knew that he was broke now, and I was paying for all the expenses. I just stole some gas from the gas station. I wasn't perfect either. I did know that Roman wasn't a role model, far from it. But it didn't really bother me anymore, since I tried to accept people the way they were, here and now. Thief or liar, so what? I'd seen Roman being honest too. We are all flawed, fucked up, beautiful and human, all at the same time.

Everyone plays their part, as if our life is being recorded on some film, the only difference is that all our scenes are acted out without a script. There was a lot of black and white about Roman, but you can't just focus on his dark side because the darkest people usually have the most glowing souls. You can't say that everyone who wears white is really good inside, either. Often it's the other way around. Roman had strength, and I admired his way of looking at the world as if it were his to roam. I was learning to let go of the preconceived notion that freedom is only achieved by material world status and possessions. I agreed to go with this guy on a road trip. I had to accept him the way he was, and he had to accept me. After our Florida incident, it felt like we finally bonded, and I didn't think we had to go through that again. The only thing missing was a couple of ladies from the twenties in long dresses dancing to Dixieland music on that steamboat.

Love by the Dirty Water

Just as I said that, we heard two girls giggling and wobbling down the boardwalk towards us. Apparently there were also drunk, smoking cigarettes and whispering to each other pointing in our direction. When they came closer, we were trying to ask them, what was so funny? The one with dark brown hair talked to us first, "Those skirts are so funny. My girlfriend and I are trying to figure out where did you get those old skirts? Are they curtains?" - and they burst out in laughter.

I tried to explain, "Well, it's a thing we decided to do." I continued, "Me and my friend we're... Well, we are on a road trip to California, and on the first day we decided to wear those ugly skirts all the way to California."

They laughed again. The other one, with dirty blonde hair and really nice tight jeans said, "Well they might be pretty smelly by now."

We chuckled, "Weeeeeeeell..."

Looking at each other, we knew a lot depended on what we said now, so we didn't know how to answer. Roman came to the rescue,

"Ladies, we are clean, intelligent men and we wash our underwear everyday. At least I do." He pointed in my direction. "He isn't wearing any."

I protested, "What do you mean?"

He continued, "Yeah you lost them after the last attack of the she-males."

I fought back. "No I didn't. I still have them on. She… He… no I didn't." I tried to explain in vain.

The girls were enjoying this scene too much and they started consulting each other about something. The dark haired one continued, "Let's make a bet, if you show us your underwear we will show you ours, but if you don't have underwear on, then you have to run up and down this boardwalk clucking like a chicken to that post over there and back." She pointed to the post on the other end of the boardwalk and they both laughed.

I thought to myself, wow, those girls are pretty daring. I really hope they are real this time and chuckled to myself.

Roman said, "Well before we show you our most dearest possessions, we should at least know your names."

The dark haired one said, "I am Janet," and the blonde answered, "Allison." Roman all of the sudden proclaimed, "This is quite a predicament. I just realized I left my wallet at the last bar we were at, do you girls want to go back there and maybe get a drink first?" I thought about it for a moment, I don't remember this bastard Roman having a

166

wallet.

Janet answered, "We already had a few drinks and now we need to get some air. Are you trying to avoid our contest?" Her eyes glistened. Janet looked like a pretty smart girl who liked to play games, just like Roman. I started questioning whether I had any underwear or not, since I didn't want to be running up and down the street butt-naked. I checked. I was ok. I looked at Roman and wasn't sure, but I guess we were put on the spot. The girls looked at us and started counting 1, 2, 3 as a sign to take off our skirts. I took my skirt off and showed my underwear. I was triumphant knowing I am not going to be the one running. I saw Roman was getting a bit uncomfortable. Perhaps for the first time since I have known him. I was thinking, oh shit, he isn't wearing any. This is going to be funny. Allison was reading my thoughts, "Uh oh, someone's going to run."

Roman turned around and walked a little towards the boardwalk rail. Then, in an instant, he pulled off his skirt and revealed his white butt to everyone and proceeded to run towards the pole at the end of the boardwalk clucking like a chicken. It happened so suddenly that everyone had their mouths open, including me, and then we just started laughing, pointing at Roman's white butt running down the street. He started singing on top of his lungs "Mama – anarkhia, Papa – stakan portveina."(Mama - anarchy, Father - a glass of port.) He ran all the way to that pole, and then he sprinted back as light as a gazelle with his privates dangling in the breeze. When he got close to us, we all turned away to protect our innocent eyes from this spectacle. Meanwhile, he was dancing around us

167

fresh as lettuce after all the drinks we had. He put the skirt back on, sat down on the bench, crossed his legs and lit a cigarette.

The girls were clapping and saying, "You guys, you are too funny!"

I kept slapping him on the back, "You are a crazy nut."
Once his breathing calmed down, he turned to girls and said; "Ladies, now it's our time to have some fun. It's your turn to reveal," and his eyes glistened. The girls got immedately shy.

We started protesting, "We showed you ours and Roman just paid the ultimate penalty. It's your turn now."

They agreed, but they said, "Ok fine, but we will just show you the color and you guys will stay where you are." We agreed. Dark haired Janet looked around to check if anyone was around, and then she pulled her tight jeans down a little bit on the side to show the color. She had on silky black underwear, and then Allison showed a little piece of her beautiful blue ones.

We gulped and moaned. Oh my god, I was like a kid in a candy store that just saw a really yummy candy, but this time I remembered what Roman said about the young bull. I decided to act like nothing happened since it was obvious the girls took interest in us. We were definitely interested in them. They were beautiful, we were all drunk, and the night was warm. I still had no ideas how those two girls ended up even talking to us, but hey when you go with the flow amazing things can happen when you least expect them.

Janet asked us, "Do you guys want to smoke a joint with us? We have a bit left."

Roman replied, "How did you know? That's exactly what we were asking this river. To send us some weed to smoke tonight, but the river said she was all out."

They giggled. Janet said to Roman, "Well you seem to be the funny one."

Roman said, "No, I just got good genes," and they made an eye connection and their eyes glistened. Meanwhile, Allison came up to me and asked, "So what is this accent I hear? Where are you from?"

I said, "Well, we are from a distant land of Mongolia, far away where the snow falls on women like the stars from the sky and makes them glow."

Allison smiled and said, "I think that's very cheesy, and beautiful at the same time. Is that from a poem?"

I answered, "No, I just made it up right now, looking at you." We looked at each other and my eyes rested completely on her for that one moment.

We walked down the boardwalk, all four of us loudly talking and discussing New Orleans. We finally found a little park and found a nice spot in the middle. We all sat cross-legged on the grass. It was a warm night. We slowly kept passing that joint around. Finally, Roman took the joint, turned it around, and motioned to Janet to join him. It was a ritual of blowing the smoke through the other end of the joint into the other person's mouth. We all knew where that led. They took a puff, started exhaling the smoke into each other's faces, and then they started making out while exhaling more smoke into each other. That looked like one smoky kiss. When they stopped, they fell backwards and started laughing. Roman started rolling sideways and Janet did the same. They kept rolling in the same direction towards the river.

Allison sat next to me, and I took a long inhale on the joint and exhaled the smoke into the warm New Orleans night. I passed it to her. She said, "You guys are so funny." I looked at her and saw in her face something really cool. She was here, next to me, and she was beautiful.

I said, "Yeah, we have been traveling for a while now. It took me a while to get used to Roman's kicks, but once I let go it's actually fun." All of a sudden I felt really stoned, I laid on my back and looked up at the stars. She did the same and I continued, "Can you imagine those stars being there for thousands, no, millions of years shinning for us? It's like someone had created the perfect backdrop for our masquerade. Have they always been there? What was the first day when the stars appeared? Who created everything?" I was tormented by those questions since I was a child and now I was asking this strange girl that I just got high with.

"I was asking the same questions," she answered. She was silent as she put her head on my shoulder. She continued, "Maybe that's why there are men and women, to look at the stars together, since it's boring to do it alone!"

I asked her, "How do you know when you are actually happy?"

She said, "My grandmother used to say this to me all the time. I am happy, here, and now, and tomorrow might never come."

I answered, "That sounds great."

We saw Roman and Janet in the distance; they were holding on to each other leaning half way over the rail looking at the Mississippi river. I looked around for a moment; we seemed to be out of the view of the streets, since there were many trees encircling the spot where we were, plus it was close to 4am. The river was in front of us and steamboats were lit up in the distance making it look like a postcard from the twenties. I don't think there was a more perfect moment. I told her, "Maybe I am a hopeless romantic after all."

We looked at each other and stopped for a moment. She whispered, "Maybe this will make you happier." She reached forward and our lips touched. She was letting me into her mouth. We were lying on the grass, and I wasn't afraid anymore. I knew this would only last a moment, and I wanted to seize it and taste it to the fullest. Our embrace was getting tighter. A question arose in my mind, "How far would she take it?" She pulled me closer and kept kissing me with those hot lips; I figured she didn't want to think. We knew we both wanted it. My hands were exploring under her shirt. She stopped me and took off her shirt completely. She didn't have a bra on, and staring at me was a pair of beautiful round breasts with pink nipples. I was in awe at this speed of events, but I didn't want to think, I wanted to live. I drank her lips, and she was planting her kisses all over me. Her hand reached out for my jeans. I was rock hard. She let me into her mouth. I moaned. The stars were listening above; they have heard human beings make love for millions of years. I was losing my mind from her soft lips around me. She climbed back up and took off her jeans. She let me take off that silky blue underwear. I was kissing her stomach and her breasts. Then finally I stopped, I looked at her and she nodded in silent agreement. I laid my t-shirt on the ground, and she sat on top of me. As we were kissing, I entered her soft warm universe. Everything stopped, and her hips started moving. We both were moving to the rhythm of our throbbing hearts. We didn't know each other, but we both needed to feel loved at that moment. We loved and kissed anxiously. I kept repeating her name, and she was saying my name over and over. She demanded that we go faster. This time I laid her down on the ground so that I could be on top. I asked her what if I come inside. She said, "Don't worry, I am on a pill." I was inside of her and I started going faster, and faster and faster, until I couldn't hold back this river of my need and urgency. She kept hugging me tighter and tighter. Her legs were clasped behind my back. She kept saying, "Please don't stop. Don't stop." She was trembling inside my arms and we were both breathing hard. I looked at her biting her lips and her beautiful naked body. As I threw my head backwards, I exploded inside of her. Her hips were rhythmically moving as I released all my love inside of her. The stars did a circle for me as I was gasping for air and the convulsions took over me.

We stayed like that for few minutes listening to the rhythm of our hearts. She leaned and whispered in my ear, "You are a poet. Don't let the world kill that inside of you." I looked at her and realized she understood.

"Ok, I promise," I whispered back. I wished that moment would never end. In that moment I knew some old wounds were healing. I felt at peace with myself for the first time in a very long time.

It started to get cold, so I put my t-shirt and underwear back on. She did the same. There was no shame and no questions. We were just lying there on the grass and hugging silently. I realized how tired I was. I felt my eyes were closing. I started dozing off so I told her I would rest here for a moment. She said go ahead. I drifted into sleep knowing there was nothing to be afraid of and no more questions to ask. The silver fog engulfed me.

I felt someone pulling the hairs on my leg. I opened my eyes. It was still dark, but dawn was looming. I saw Roman studying my leg and pulling my leg hairs one by one. I quickly sat up, "Ouch! That hurts, you ass."

I looked around for Allison. She wasn't there. Roman looked at me and said, "Come on let's go you Mississippi bum. Look at you, lying here by yourself, in the middle of the park without a girl or your pants, I mean skirt. By the way, where is your skirt?"

I said, "Dude come on I am cold. Where is it?"

He said, "I don't know maybe it's decorating that tree." I looked at the tree, and my skirt was hanging from the branch up high on a tree. It looked funny. I was going to say you are a jerk, but instead I just asked, "Have you seen Allison?"

Roman answered with a question, "Who? Ah, the naughty girl someone fell in love with last night? Oh yeah, her and Janet both went back to their hotel somewhere on Bourbon street. I walked them back a little bit, but I had to return since I couldn't leave the sleeping beauty here all by herself."

I was smiling, "Dude, what happened. That was like the best night ever. Did you make it with Janet?"

Roman said, "Gentleman never tells, but I can tell you it seems like they will remember our skirts for a long time."

We both laughed, "Ha ha ha."

I added, "This time we finally scored with the real ladies."

We laughed even louder. I took my skirt off of the tree after few unsuccessful attempts with a stick and finally put it on. It was a cold morning so I said, "All right, Let's go man. This ground is uncomfortable. I guess let's go sleep in the car."

He answered, "Yes our hotel le royal awaits us." I officially looked like a bum now, but I couldn't care less. I was happy. We walked back to Bourbon Street.

Bourbon Street resembled a war zone with trash and bottles everywhere. We needed rest, so we went to pass out in the car.

Later in the morning it was the same routine. First, we had to find some food and coffee. We stumbled inside a European looking café. After a second cup of coffee, I felt much better. I realized it was here that life happens, while you are busy having a hangover and over- analyzing every little detail. It happens right here. The mellow sounds of jazz somewhere in the distance made me realize again where we were. The light came forth from the blazing sun into our lives and onto the streets where the debauchery occurred the night before. Now the streets were quiet, and somewhere in the distance someone had just opened the windows of one of the bars.

We had croissants with egg and cheese. It was good to give our stomachs a break and have some real good food for a change. The fact that New Orleans used to be a French Colony really made an impact on the place. The European architecture, lamp posts, and the horse carriages made me feel as if we were somewhere in France in the 1800's. Roman wanted to keep moving. It seemed he didn't want to stay in one place for more than a day. I really started to like New Orleans. I promised myself I would come back and explore next time.

Driving out of Louisiana, we got to see the real swampland. As far as you could see, on the left and right of the highway, the swamps were claiming their territory. I stared at the swamps and I could have sworn an imaginary swamp creature was sitting on a far away piece of floating swamp bush and waving at us. He had an old French hat on and instead of feet he had a fish tail with scales. The sun was shining over no man's land and the white lane was our guide out of Louisiana. Creedence Clearwater Revival was on the stereo playing my favorite song, "I Put a Spell on You." New Orleans definitely put a spell on me. The swamp blues spell.

Chapter 10

Texas

We are not commies!

We are hippies!

Don't Mess With Texas

The next state was Texas. Since it was smack in the middle of the United States, it was considered to be the heart of the country. When we rode into Texas, a huge road sign greeted us with a Texas star and a cowboy boot. From our car window we could see cowboys with Stetson hats driving their pickup trucks. It seemed as if it was obligatory to wear them when you drive no matter if your hat fit inside or not. We got hungry real quick, so we turned off the road to get something to eat and there it was, the famous sign: *Don't Mess With Texas* and the word *Mess* was crossed out and *Fuck* was written right above it. We decided to take that advice literally and not fuck with the Texans since they probably wouldn't understand our joke, and might have few rifles in their pickup trucks. Our cut down flags against their rifles, we didn't stand a chance. We decided to get some food at Burger King. Every idiot was welcome at Burger King.

We are not commies! We are hippies!

After filling our stomachs with processed American food and driving out of the parking lot we saw a sign that read *Splash Kingdom,* on top of the water park with long wavy water slides right next to the highway. We decided to go there since we were sweating and the heat was becoming unbearable. We changed into our swimming trunks and with screams and giggles resembling 5-year-old girls' we went sliding with the rest of the kids. Our long hairy legs were occasionally sticking out of the water as the slides were turning us over on the way down.

After about an hour of water sliding we got changed and headed back to the car. We stood by the car rapidly speaking Russian as we noticed an older man standing by listening to our conversation. We were pretty sure he didn't understand us, but he was curious to find out who these foreigners were. He looked like an older typical Texan: grey hair, a black baseball hat with admiral fleet symbols, beige slacks and a polo shirt. He spoke slower because he was a southerner and he had nowhere to rush to. He asked us where we were from and where were we going. We told him we were from New York going to California and then he asked, "Where was the foreign accent from?" When we told him we were from Russia his expression changed. His eyes turned into a TV set; years of propaganda, fire of the Cold War era lighting up in his pupils, anti-communist slogans, radio broadcasting nuclear threats, newspapers with enemy slogans, Eisenhower delivering a speech, and Brezhnev mumbling that we will annihilate them. He saw us as intruders, warriors infiltrating his land to conquer and to take over the very principles of liberty and freedom. The muscles on his face tightened up and we asked him, "Are you ok, pap?" I used the fifties way of referring to an older man that Henry Miller used in his books. He shook up as if he was awakening from his dream; he looked at our happy faces, two dudes that really couldn't care less about politics, nationalities, or nuclear energy. Just to reassure him, I added, "We are not commies. We are hippies. We are just looking for good times!"

I noticed the fire of propaganda receding and slowly dying out, as a smile of acceptance and forgiveness came back to him. He chuckled, "Well you boys look like you sure are having fun here in Texas!"

We said, "Yeah, we are on a road trip. Texas is great, especially those water slides in this heat."

He loosened up, "Well boys that's good to hear." Then he looked away into the distance and said, "I want to give you a small present," and walked towards his pickup truck. We looked at each other, perplexed a bit as to what that might be. A few minutes later he came back with a little cloth rolled up and handed it to us. We opened it up and it was a confederate flag. I was about to start protesting, but there was a look of pride on his face and he continued, "I want you to have it boys, so you remember Texas." I thought for a moment, does everyone in Texas drive around with those flags in their cars, but hey a present is a present.

As we were saying goodbye we shook his calloused hand. I could see a tear on the old man's cheek. It was good to see that we served a purpose – helping him see what he thought was his enemy in a different light. We thanked him for the gift. In the end, the most notable moments in history were when warriors on both sides gave up their weapons and embraced one another in the simplest of human gestures.

As we were pulling out we noticed a Texan cop in his car eyeing us, as if trying to figure out what we were up to. On the side of it there was a golden star and word that sent a chill up my spine, "SHERIFF!" That sheriff noticed our license plates, and he definitely was about to check out our purpose on his turf. Roman looked at me and said, "Ne ssat'!" (Don't piss!) "I am not!" I lied. Roman explained the best way to eliminate curiosity is to be the first to reveal your intentions, and that's what we are going to do. I was wondering what gangster movie that came from... The Godfather? As we pulled up I saw a Texan sheriff in all his glory: a sheriff's cowboy hat, double chin hanging over his shirt collar, a bag of Dunkin Donuts in the window. It seemed like the police cliché was still going strong. He looked like he had short patience. He was chewing and looking at us suspiciously, the same way you look at criminals when you know they are going to tell you a lie.

I pulled my facial muscles into a smile as huge as I could, and with an innocent face I asked him with overemphasized amount of cheeriness, "Excuse me Sir, would you know how to get back on the highway?" – he looked inside our car and saw Roman with his best smile and his little musketeer mustache. Roman's instructions kicked in, *Let him know what we are doing so they will lose interest in us*. I continued. "We are on a road trip to California and we are a little lost, and we are trying to get out of Texas."

That started working and he started to lose interest in a couple of innocent idiots like us, so he just pointed his fat finger towards the direction of a highway and said, "Just get on Route 10 it will take you right outta Texas."

I said, "Thank you very much, sir."

Roman continued in his most friendly voice, "Have a nice day now!"

As we were driving away we also wished him to have some good pork chops, lots of doughnuts, roasted goose and to stuff his face until he dropped.

Chapter 11

Mexican Amigo

Sometimes good hombres drive me.

How you say it in English?

Our third passenger, Mexican "Amigo"

We were still driving through Texas and the next big city on our way was Houston. Driving down the *American Dream* highway we saw ranches and grasslands with free roaming cattle. The cows were chewing on their grass, building up fat, to be slaughtered later, sliced, cooked and eaten in one of the fine country cooking restaurants that served famous Angus beef burgers. Some cat in a cowboy hat would be whining about his lost cowgirl through the little speakers of the restaurant and life would go on pretty much unchanged. The only thing that was missing was bunch of Indians galloping after some buffaloes.

We had about one hundred and fifty miles left to Houston. We were out of fuel so we stopped at a gas station that looked like a thousand other gas stations. After we filled up the car we were goofing around with the apples we bought at the rest area supermarket. As we are eating them we were throwing the pits and leftovers at each other. I noticed some Latin dude walking over to us and when he started asking us for some change I told him we didn't have any, which was true, since all the change we had Roman gave to John back in Florida. Roman turned to him and said, "We got some apples though. You want one?" He nodded, so Roman threw him an apple. The Latin American guy started crunching away at his apple. He seemed hungry. I turned to look at him closely; he was a Latin homeboy with a mullet, jean shorts to the knee, a white tank top, old white sneakers and white socks pulled all the way up.

Roman asked him, "So where are you going?"

He answered, "I go to Dallas to see my hermana."

Roman continued, "How are you getting there?"

The guy replied, "I walk."

We stopped throwing apples around and just stared at him. I asked, "What do you mean you are walking? On the highway?"

He looked away in the direction of the highway and continued; "Sometimes good hombres drive me. How you say in English?"

Roman asked, "Hitchhike?"

The dude agreed, "Yeah, I hitch-hike."

Roman continued, "Where are you walking from?"

He answered, "From Louisiana." He took out a brush and started combing his hair. He looked like a person who didn't have it easy. He looked like he worked hard labor, but in his small arms and legs there was strength and a will to survive and to rebel. I looked at his long jean shorts and at his tank top and started noticing that he didn't have anything on him. He was probably walking with nothing but his hairbrush. After he was done combing his hair he was just standing there looking at us through his half closed eyes and waiting for whatever fate had prepared for him.

Roman asked, "What's your name?"

He answered, "Jose," and Roman told him our names.

We shook hands in silence. I was hoping he would keep on walking wherever he was going, and right as I was thinking it, Roman asks him, "Amigo, why don't you come with us. We can take you as far as Houston and then you can hitchhike up the highway towards Dallas?" I couldn't believe Roman just asked him that. I was against crazy Roman's idea. This guy was from God knows where. Maybe I should say Devil knows where and God is clueless. We were looking at each other; this guy didn't look like he could even be trusted. I didn't like him, and he obviously was not really fond of me either. I hated Roman's games. I know we drove John fifteen minutes down the street but driving to another city was too much.

Moreover, I was furious at how he just offered a ride to this dude without even asking me. I motioned to Roman, "Dude we have to talk."

He turned to me and said with a grimace, "About what?"

I was beyond pissed, "Come on man. Let's go to the side over here." Roman obviously didn't want to talk so he walked slowly.

I spoke fast in low tone, "Dude are you serious? You are about to give a ride to a total stranger. Man, we don't even know this guy. Last time we were giving John a lift down the street, I almost passed out from heatstroke. What if this guy steals our stuff or the car? Man that's all we got!" I tried to be cool about many things already, but this was pushing it. I looked back at Jose. He was sitting on the curb kind of waiting carelessly, looking over the horizon expecting the sky to pull out a knife out or something sharp and hurt him, so he was studying the sky before it did.

It was Roman's turn to get pissed off, "Why do you always have to have a problem everytime I want to have some fun and help some people? All you care about is how you feel and scared of what can happen. Nothing is going to happen. Just think of other people for once and you are forgetting, it's my fucking car. Remember the first rule?" Roman looked back at him and then he turned to me quickly, "Come on Dimon, this guy is all right; he is just a little hombre. Haven't you heard of giving rides to hitchhikers? He has got nothing on him. It's not a big deal, we are just going to give him a ride and that's all. We'll let him out on the way to Dallas and last time you didn't pass out because we gave someone a ride you passed out because you didn't have any water."

He started walking away. He had a screwed up way of looking at things, but he had a point. I started thinking maybe I was overreacting again. The guy was walking and we were driving so we could help him. I squeezed some compassion out of myself, but I wasn't cool with him driving with us further than Houston.

I yelled back at Roman, "Alright, no further than Houston!"

Roman wanted to end it so he agreed, "Yeah. Yeah."

We walked back to Jose sitting on the curb. Roman told him about our decision, or more like his decision.

Jose looked at me and asked Roman, "You sure? I mean, if it's ok with your boy, 'cause you know I am ok."

Roman answered, "Yeah, no problems, Can you drive a stick shift?" He nodded in agreement.

Roman added, "You will be our second driver, since every time Dmitry drives the whole car smells like burnt clutch."

I turned around to him and said, "Alright man, only up to Houston, but after that we are going to California!"

He looked at me and then at Roman and replied with a smile, "Gracias amigos. Muchas gracias."

We made space for him at the back, and now we had a third person in our car, which seemed completely out of balance since it had only been me and Roman this whole time. I couldn't shake off the nervousness. Jose was just quiet and he was looking out of the window studying the road on which he was about to keep on walking if we hadn't picked him up.
I tried a little conversation to loosen things up, "Where you from?" I asked.

"Tijuana" he answered

I continued, "Long time here?" I was trying to be tough, by cutting sentences short, but he sounded bored.

He answered the same way, short and to the point, "Ten years."

I answered, "Cool." It was going nowhere and it was awkward trying to start a conversation with someone you don't know. Music was playing low; Roman was fixated on the road and kept quiet.

Jose leaned forward to the front seat and asked us, "You hombres drive long time?"

Roman said, "Yeah about week and a half. Not too long, this is my fifth time crossing the country. It's peaceful driving back and forth. This time I got this juvenile delinquent with me though," and he nodded at me.

I reacted instantly, "Fuck you man. You are the criminal and the thief here."

They laughed at my expense. That kind of pissed me off as well. Roman reacted, "Relax man, I am just kidding! Oh I just realized I never told you about the rule number two on the road. If someone jokes on your account, next time you joke on their account and never, ever show that you are hurt by anyone's jokes."

I was quiet for a while and then I asked Jose, "Why are you walking to see your sister?" – I continued, "I mean, why do you live in separate cities? I have a sister too. She goes to school in Washington DC. I drive up to see her sometimes."

Jose got quiet for a while as he was looking out of the window then he leaned over from the back seat and said in a softer voice, but loud enough so we could hear him, "Mi hermana, she is in prison man. It was her birthday last week. I walk to see her." That phrase was like a cold reality on top of our high school party cake, and the serious tone settled in the car.

I looked at Roman with a look of serious disapproval and with the following thoughts, "Great! This guy has got a sister in jail, maybe he is a con himself, and he is riding with us in the car. This will be fun."

Roman got very interested. He started asking so what was she in for. The guy was quiet for another few minutes and then he spoke softly,

"For drugs man," - and he looked out of the window. Roman was silent now and looked straight ahead.

I didn't like the guy, and he apparently was still not feeling sympathetic towards me either. We ended up not carrying on the conversation, so the words were left hanging in the air. An hour later the clouds were gathering all around us, the sky was turning grey. I put on my favorite Doors song, "Riders on the Storm." I felt like we were *the riders on the storm*, because a huge rainstorm was approaching.

> *Riders on the storm*
> *There is a killer on the road*
> *His Brain is swarming like a toad*
> *If you give this man a ride sweet family will die.*
> *Riders on the storm*

Hole in the Nail

The thunder was increasing, and the rain started pouring heavily. It was difficult to drive, so we stopped at the first fast food joint to get some food. As we were getting out of the car, Jose was holding the door, and I noticed his fingernail on his right thumb was significantly longer than the others. It had a hole in it. It made me feel uneasy. I wasn't sure what it was for or why he had it, but I really wanted to ask him.

"Hey Jose, why do you have a hole in your nail?"

He acted like he didn't hear what I said. I repeated my question when we sat down behind the table, and he pretended he didn't hear me again. He just got up and left to go to the bathroom. I got pissed off when people ignored me. I turned to Roman and asked, "Did you see his nail? What the hell is that for? Why does he have a hole in his nail?"

Roman shrugged his shoulders, "I don't know. Why don't you ask him yourself?" I said that I did and he didn't answer. Roman said, "Well maybe he doesn't want to tell you."

When he got back, I already had a grudge on Jose and decided not to speak to him. I thought, if he doesn't want to answer my questions, he didn't deserve my attention. We ate our sandwiches in silence, of which we had to break off a half for our little buddy so he could eat too. After we got back on the road Roman, and Jose were talking about Mexico. I went to sleep at the back, but I could hear their conversation. Roman asked Jose after few minutes, "What's with the hole in the nail? My friend wanted to know."

Jose looked out of the window, and at that moment I half awoke to hear his reply. He turned back to Roman and put his thumbnail to his nose and sniffed through it. "Cocaina," he answered. He explained further, "Test the drogas man; before you make bags."

Roman asked with a hint, "You got any on you now?"

Jose replied, "No Amigo, I am finito with drugs man."

Roman said, "Good."

I was about to start judging Jose. I wasn't sure why we had to pick him up and why was he in the car with us, but instead I laid there thinking with my eyes open. I didn't trust the outside world. I thought about John from Florida. I was way more relaxed about that situation, but somehow every new thing that came along, instead of opening up and trusting the flow, I freaked out immediately. I knew that my fear came from years and years of growing up in New York and watching my family go through the same motion of expecting the world to hurt you if you open up to it, especially when you are an immigrant. I realized one simple and yet profound truth; the way we are today has everything to do with what our parents have been telling us our whole lives. Now that I was here, I realized my parent's views were a part of my view of the world and how I perceived it. I was taught to judge from the beginning, but there was always a possibility to change how you feel about the world around you. If you just let go of someone else's point of view, and acquire a new trust in what's coming, things will be very different. Now that I look back on those moments, over and over Roman's openness was just his way of saying I trust the world the way it is and whatever it sends my way, good or bad. Those that fear it build up walls to protect themselves out of fear, but essentially every person we meet is our reflection that comes in many forms and shapes. We need to accept it the way it is. Even though that other person wears a different body, has a different name, place of birth, origin, country and language we need to accept it as part of us, without judgment. Deep inside we are all made from the particles of the same universe that connects us all deep within.

I thought about Jose, and why he was here with us. He was a lone wolf on the road, without a plan and without a buck. He just was living in this moment and whatever it had to offer. He was raised on the streets as a thug, trained to survive, and walking across the states wasn't a problem for him. Although being an ex-drug dealer definitely teaches you things, but the reality was thus: He was walking alone on the highway without any means to an end.

Strangely enough, I started feeling compassion for our amigo and for his silent ways. All those thoughts and emotions came rushing through me. I had a college degree and even though my life now was chaotic, who is to say it will always stay like this, plus my sister went to college and she wasn't in jail. How could I be so judgmental about someone who had nothing? Tears rolled down my face as I stared into the night behind the windshield. An old wound was healing a little more, as I heard Allison's words in my ear, "Don't let the world kill the poet inside." I decided that one day I would write down everything I went through on this road trip because for some reason I had to be here and experience it.

Roman and Jose were talking about the road, and how he was hitchhiking across Louisiana. He was walking for a few hours before he came up on the rest area where we picked him up. Roman asked Jose what his plans were once he visited his sister. He said he didn't know. He probably would go back, or stick around and look for work somewhere. It was my time to be sarcastic, "Or you can just road trip across the country and ask people for money for gas like Roman over here." Roman wasn't happy when I poked fun at him for not having any dough of his own, so I was the one laughing now.

All of a sudden, Roman asked, "Jose, why don't you come with us to California, huh? I mean if you want to see your sister, that's one thing. We will respect it, but maybe you can get a job in Los Angeles or Portland. I mean you can't be responsible for your sister's choices, but you could start your life again. Once she gets out you can come and pick her up in your brand new car. Think about it. It's your chance to travel basically for free."

Jose paused. He was thinking. "I don't know, amigo. Mi hermana is my blood. I always say Feliz Cumple to her." He went silent and looked at the road contemplating. After about five minutes of silence, he continued, "I got a cousin in Oregon. He always tell me there is good trabajo there, and mi hermana tell me she wants me to be good and find a job." This time, I held back because my head was rushing forward with obvious objections, but then I decided to trust Roman. I got tired of protesting and plus, my compassion grew for our amigo.

Roman continued, "I am sure it will be ok with Dmitry over there," and he nodded at me.

I said, "Sure man, I don't mind. It's all good."

The emotions on Jose's face were visible; he was making decisions, and he was fighting it, the little man's life was either going to go one way or another according to what he decided.

We stopped at the intersection of Route 10 and Route 45 that led to Dallas and looked at Jose. Roman said, "Let us know what you want to do. If you want us to let you out now or if you want to, you are welcome to ride with us." Roman turned down the music, "You decide man."

Jose looked at the road leading to Dallas, and then he looked ahead. It looked like he made a decision, "If it's ok with you, I go to California amigos. I send postcard to mi hermana to say feliz cumples. I help you drive this car no problema." We agreed. We stopped on the curb and repacked the car to make a sleeping space for one more person in the back. I sucked at driving a stick shift. It was a good thing there was one more driver so Roman could rest because he drove most of the way. We got back on the road, and now we were a bizarre trio: two Russians and one Mexican dude, an ex-coke dealer.

Senor Panza's Rancho

Jose was driving, Roman was sleeping in the passenger's seat, and I on the back seat. Later, when Roman woke up, he started to ask Jose inquisitively if he knew anyone to get weed from on the road, since we were out of grass. Jose felt like he wanted to repay us in some way, so he told us about a rancho around San Antonio, Texas along Route 10. If we wanted to go, he could take us there.

The whole idea seemed a little crazy to me, but I was up for it this time around since we ran out of weed a few days ago. I looked at Roman and said, "Dude davai. (Let's do it.) I don't mind man. Let's do it."

Roman screamed out, "Hell yeah, baby! Now we talking!" He turned to Jose and said in a deep alien sounding voice, "Jose take me to your dealer." Roman laughed at his own joke while slapping his thighs. Then he put on a reggae song on and started to sing, imitating the accent, "Are we going to get smoked up tonight? Are we going to get fucked up tonight?" What's worse is that Russians can't dance reggae or do a Jamaican accent very well, but hey, we can try.

We drove for a while down Route 10 to San Antonio, Texas. There, we got off the highway and went down Route 90 to a town called Eagle Pass. We figured it was on the border with Mexico because we saw so many Mexicans on the streets. We drove down some small local roads, and then we finally came to a stop next to the metal gates and read the sign: *Sr. Panza's Rancho*. When we got out of the car, we saw a large fenced grass field and animals grazing here and there.

Jose went to the intercom to inform that we were coming. He came back and the metal gate opened by itself as a sign to drive inside. Roman immediately asked, "What's this place man? Looks interesting."

Jose answered, "Someone I used to work for."

I held back any comments and just tried to go with the flow. We drove slowly down the dirt road and saw two llamas standing chewing on grass with their ears perked up. Llama - a Peruvian farm animal that was a mix between a sheep and a camel, only smaller and without a hump. That was a random sight to see, a llama in the middle of Texas. Dirt road turned to pavement, and well-groomed bushes surrounded the road on both sides. The road finally curved, and in the far left we saw an impressive two-story, bright orange hacienda with columns up front, a big chimney towering over, and Italian styled white balconies. We made our way around the circular driveway to the front door.

I noticed two unpleasant looking men suited in black coming out of the house and standing by the front door. They were built like brick houses, and they were wearing dark sunglasses. I wasn't getting a good feeling about this. I let Roman and Jose know about it, but Jose replied, "Don't worry amigo, I know Sr. Panza good."

As we stopped the car in front of the front door Jose got out of the car and waited silently. Two security guys were eyeing him suspiciously. Jose didn't say anything. He just waited as usual. The front door opened and another casually dressed Mexican guy came outside. He walked up to

Jose, reached his hand out saying in Spanish, "Jose, mi amigo. ¿Cuántos años?" (Jose, my friend, how many years?)

Jose replied, "Mucho tiempo, Senor Panza." (Long time, Senor Panza.)

Senor Panza seemed much younger than I expected. I remembered from watching Russian movies about the mafia that mob bosses were supposed to be mean and big, but this guy seemed young, pleasant and relaxed. I calmed down a bit. As long as this guy was in a good mood, we got nothing to worry about from the two huge security guards. As if the guy read my mind, he motioned to the big guys by the door. The two brick houses went inside the house. Roman was eating this scene up with his eyes, and I was kind of curious myself about this friend of Jose. We got out of the car to greet the owner. He was wearing flip-flops, cut off jean shorts, a short sleeve Hawaii shirt, and a pleasant smile under his aviator sunglasses. The only really mafia looking expensive item he wore was an expensive looking huge shiny watch on his left wrist. It probably had diamonds in it, but I couldn't tell.

I didn't think Jose would know people like this, but I guess when you are in a drug business you get to know where the supply comes from. Jose presented us and said, "Senor Panza, meet my amigos Russos Americanos Roman and Dmitry. They drive me to California."

We exchanged handshakes and he said in perfect English, "Guys, just call me Joe. I grew up here, in the USA. Jose worked for me in the past. If you are friends with Jose, you are my friends."

It was Roman's turn to speak, "Joe, what a great place you got here. I don't think I have ever seen a llama in my life."

Joe was wiping his hands, "Oh, that. Yeah, I got those in Peru. I thought it was the most intelligent animal, although watch out. You don't want her to spit at you. You might drown. They are just like camels." He looked at our attire and started laughing, "Why are you guys wearing granny skirts?" - and he let out a good belly laugh.

Roman replied, "No, we are challenging normality. We wear these skirts to fight against oppression of the mind by the roles society assigned to us."

I added, "It even got us out of being arrested."

Joe answered, "No shit? If that keeps you away from being arrested, I should try wearing one," he was still enjoying a good laugh about our appearance as he motioned for us to come inside the house.

We walked inside Joe's house and stepped on the marble floors. Roman and I were awe struck. In between the car, the road, and an occasional cheap motel, we had not entered a house of such luxury and impeccable taste. There were black and white leather couches, huge paintings, tall vases and bear skin carpets on the floor. In the middle of the room, there was a big fireplace. Above it there was a painting of a reclining nude. I believed it was Francisco Goya by the style, but I wasn't quite sure. I admired this guy's style and appreciation for the arts.

Two burly security guys were standing next to the entrances to the other two rooms and watched our every move. All of sudden, from around the corner, two Doberman Pinschers ran out from behind the corner and headed straight towards us. Roman and I looked for something to grab in our defense cursing, "Blya, Blya, Blya." (Fuck, Fuck, Fuck) Before the dogs reached us Joe put his two fingers in his mouth and whistled really loud. He raised his right arm up and let out a strong yell, "Halt!" The dogs stopped running, sat down and put their heads down in obedience. Joe said to us, "I apologize for that guys. They are just puppies in training." We gulped and stopped hugging the white statue next to us for protection. The two burly security guys smiled at our fear with the corners of their mouths. That was probably the most enjoyment they got for the day.

Joe continued, "I can never trust anyone that comes to my house unless they are friends. I have got to make sure I keep my private property well protected.".

Joe turned towards Jose and asked him, "So what was that you wanted?"

Jose answered, "Mi amigos, want to buy smoke for the road. We were close. I remember about you." It was obvious Jose didn't want to be there, but he was doing us a favor.

Joe said, "Oh yeah sure. It's a perfect time. I just got a new shipment, so you guys will help me sample it." He started walking towards the room on the left, and then he turned around to us and pointed towards the glass doors on the far right and said, "Why don't you guys wait for me by the pool? Take a dip if you want. It's over there."

Jose answered, "No we wait here," but Joe insisted and said, "Jose, the boys probably want to take a dip in a swimming pool, plus you are my guests, and I haven't had any guests for a while. It's always business and no pleasure for me. Just go and wait for me," Joe insisted. We nodded and went to the pool.

We walked towards the glass doors and through a carpeted room with a huge billiards table in the middle. One of the big burly guys was following us. When we opened the doors, we saw a nice size pool with bright blue water in it. Water fountains in shapes of Italian statues were surrounding the pool with water coming out of every one of them. It was a really picturesque pool, straight out of a Vogue magazine. We noticed a woman swimming at the far end of the pool. We sat down on beach chairs around a white table, took out our cigarettes, and lit them.

When the woman saw us sitting down, she swam towards us with a look of mistrust. When she swam up close she asked, "Who are you?"

Roman answered, "We are friends with Joe. He told us to wait for him here."

Mistrusting us, she glanced at one of the brick houses by the door. He silently nodded in agreement in return, probably meant the boss approved.

She said, "Ok, I am almost out. Give me ten minutes."

I said, "Hey no worries. Take your time. We are the intruders here." She warmed up and smiled, showing off her pearly whites. She was tanned, had blonde hair, and she was wearing a white, tight-fitting swimming suit that made her look as if she came with this picturesque pool.

At that moment, Joe came out of the house with a few vials in each hand. He said, "Ah, I see you already met Krystal." He turned towards her and said, "Krystal cupcake, meet my friends, " – and he introduced us one by one.

We waved at her and she smiled back at us again. He proceeded to sit down and announced, "I brought few things for us to try." He took out a long silver smoking pipe and filled it with some weed from the first vial and said, "This is Silver Haze, my friends." He looked at the label and read, "Very smooth taste with a hint of spice." After taking a hit, he passed the small pipe around, allowing us to take a long deep hit each. Jose made a sign that he didn't want any. Joe shrugged his shoulders and said, "As you wish Jose. Esto es pura." (This is Pure.) Joe opened another vial and read the label first, "Train Wreck - Sweet and Tangy." He joked, "Train Wreck? Ha!" He filled the pipe again, took a hit himself, and then passed it to us for a second round. We each took a long hit and exhaled the smoke in one big cloud.

I started coughing, and a thought appeared in my head, "Where the hell are we?" A little voice inside answered, "Who cares man? We are chilling." I questioned myself in my head, "What is this voice inside that I constantly hear?", and the voice answered, "I am you. I have been you and will always be you!" I sat there, a bit perplexed, but that relaxed me at the same time. I guess it was good to have a quick conversation with yourself.

Krystal was walking up the stairs to exit the pool. As if in slow motion, she came out of the water like a creature from another planet, oozing sexuality and unattainable pleasure. We couldn't help but to stare at her. Every sway of her hips was a calculated movement. She ran her fingers along her hair, and we all stopped breathing. I started doubting that she was real. I wiped my eyes and looked at Roman. He was playing with his mustache, also transfixed. Joe himself stopped what he was doing and was also staring at his woman's hips. Only Jose looked away, sitting a few chairs away from us. Joe took a drag on the pipe and exhaling a big cloud of smoke leaned over to us and said, "Pretty hot, huh guys? That's my Texan beauty."

She picked up the towel and finally said jokingly, "Can I help you gentlemen?"

We all stopped staring and looked away, each mumbling sorry. She put her towel around her waist and walked towards the house. She stopped next to Joe and said, "See you later baby. Don't take too long."

Joe said, "Of course sugar," and he gave her a slight slap on her butt.

He turned around to us and said with a feeling of content, "That's what I call success gentlemen." Then he refilled our tasting pipe and passed it around the third time with those words, "And this is White Widow. The crème of the crop."

We took a drag each and sat there transfixed. I exhaled, realizing I was really stoned and I discovered another interesting thing. My vision became rectangular, as if my mind was observing where I was through a rectangular TV screen. When I turned my head left or right my TV vision was delayed and it took a while for me to focus again. It was phenomenal. Roman exhaled and said, "This is really good Joe." I couldn't even speak.

Joe proceeded to open the last little vial and made three perfect long lines of white powder on the table and said, "No tasting goes perfect without a little powder for our noses. Here is the finest Colombian cocaine that anybody can get in the state of Texas. How do I know that? Because, I tried it all and this is the best I tell you." He rolled a hundred dollar bill, sniffed one line and then passed the bill to me. I looked at the bill. That was equal to four fill ups for our car. I looked at the long white line in front of me and thought, "I really shouldn't, but fuck it I am already here." I snorted that long line of cocaine. I felt like a light bulb went off in my head, and bombs started exploding in my brain. The next moment I felt a shot of energy in my heart, and I became really focused and relaxed at the same time.

Roman proceeded to do the same only before he sniffed his line he said, "Come to daddy my little snow white," apparently that was his key phrase. We all leaned back on the comfortable reclining chairs with pillows for our heads. I thought this was the life. Water was glistening in the pool and light electronic music started playing through the speakers. I looked at Jose and then at Roman and laughed a really good laugh. I felt great being this stoned, but there was one paranoid thought that crawled into my head. I hope we don't do anything stupid now, otherwise those security guys over there will have our guts for lunch.

Joe smiled, looked at us and asked Roman, "What was that we were talking about when you came in?"

Roman pulled on his little mustache and said, "How our skirts are ruining the image of normality in the people we meet."

Joe said, "I applaud your style Roman. This is precisely the reason why we were bound to meet today. Because we challenge normality when they are trying to hang it on us like the overcoats." Joe turned towards me and asked, "And what happened to your hand?"

I said, "I broke it over the face of someone in Florida who told me he didn't like the style of the swimming trunks I was wearing."

Joe said, "What do you mean?"

I answered, "Well he was dissing my short European style swimming trunks, and I didn't like his American baggy swim shorts. You know, the ones to your knee. We played a game of Russian roulette, only with our punches. He lost, but I broke my arm on his face."

Joe laughed and slapped his knees with his hands, "Puta Madre Dmitry."

I smiled and continued, "Roman even bought me a sticker after that, *Why Be Normal*?"

Joe said, "Yeah man, why be normal? That's fucking brilliant. Now let me ask you what does the word *normal* mean?" Without waiting for our answer he continued, "That's a label created by people who segregate black from white. What's the root of that word? *Norm* - means a certain set of standards, a pattern of social behavior, set forth by a certain group. Therefore *Normal* means a person that follows the *Norm*. Moreover, that person follows the rules set forth by a certain group of people. Let me ask you who is that fucking group of people? Where are they? I don't know them. Do you know them? I haven't seen that first person that said this is normal and that is abnormal." Roman was nodding with his head. I was listening attentively and this talk was firing me up. Joe continued, "Normal is like a big marketing campaign. They wave the *Normal* flag to attract people and then they get those people to buy into the norm before they even know what it is. Because someone they respect in the community said 'this is *Normal,*' and therefore it is automatically accepted by everyone, and that over there, that's not *Normal,* therefore it's shunned."

Metallica's song *Master of Puppets* came through the speakers and he continued, "Let me tell you what's normal for my nationality: the Mexicans. Do you think it's the president that runs the country? It's the Mexicans that run this whole damn country. Mexicans are the underdogs. They work in every possible shitty job. Mexicans work at vegetable stores, restaurants, construction, cleaning houses, babysitting; they work everywhere man. Mexicans are what makes this country move forward. It's normal for a Mexican to work six days a week, to watch soccer and then have barbeques on the weekends at local state parks drinking beer and playing soccer with his friends. Now, do I want this normality for myself? Do I want to be a normal Mexican? Hell fucking no! I am the anti-Mexican. I am the lord of my own life, man. I am the master of puppets," and he pounded himself on the chest.

"Let me tell you, it goes back even earlier, way back when you were at school. Here is a great example for you. A certain set of students were cool and the other kids weren't. Those kids that sat at the back of the classroom and didn't know how to fit in, or weren't interested in fitting in, they were called *abnormal.* Meanwhile those kids at the back of the classroom were the ones that had dreams about flying, building spaceships and developing new formulas that govern science. Those kids grew up into people that are really creating an impact on our society and *normal* popular kids at school ended up fucking advertising *normal* for the future generations. *Normal* is a plague that needs to die away. It already fucked up our previous generations. Now it's time for the abnormal kids to stand up and say, 'Why should I be normal? Why follow the dogma that for the most was written by the government to control and to manipulate the masses."

He stopped and took a sip of water. We sat there staring at him. He said, "It's the fucking Churh that created this *normal* campaign. To enslave and to control by scaring people with Satan if they don't confirm to their normality. I know! I went to catholic school and those concepts of Lord the Savior and the Satan are deeply embedded into my brain." He was in rage by now, he took out his gold chain with a gold cross on it and held it up to show us, "Do you think Jesus Christ was normal? He was a weirdo, a shaman, and a magician. He turned fucking water into wine and healed the blind; can you believe he did that? Do you see anyone doing that now, two thousand and something years later? He was the anti-*normal,* and people followed and worshiped him because he gave them hope and then the *normal* killed him for fear of becoming too popular. Then after they killed him they proclaimed him to be a savior and converted others into following him. Notice the ultimatum: follow this abnormal guy with a beard, who turned wine into water and cured the sick, but don't try to be abnormal yourself. People got it all fucking wrong from the beginning. Everyone should be Jesus if they allowed themselves. People are naturally drawn to everything that's not *normal,* but they have manipulated us since the beginning into accepting the *norm.* All of a sudden, Joe jumped up from his chair and yelled. "Do you think God was normal? GOD – the creator of all that we don't even see, and yet we say, *Oh My God* every minute, as if it's a normal thing." He sat down.

Roman got up and started clapping slowly, "Wow Joe. Can I marry you?"

I liked what Joe was saying. Jose just kept staring at the floor.

He got up and continued, "Look at me, I make my living by getting people high. Do you think that, for one second, I don't think about the effect it has on our society? I fucking think about it all the time. I am getting people fucked up. Some of them shouldn't even be touching drugs, but guess what? I find peace in one thought, by getting people high, they will make a crack in their own reality, and through that crack they will see a glimpse of a different world. The real world, my friends, is not even real. It's an extraordinarily complex place governed by the simple rules of energy, but instead, we are all part of this *Truman Show*. Even after that movie came out, people are still continuing to go along with the script. Why? I ask you." Joe looked straight at us. "Because, it's easier to accept what you have than to strive for something different. Now drugs, they just show you what's behind the veil. What is really behind the veil? For each person it looks different, but in fact it is the same thing. I just hope that people have enough brains to stop doing drugs when it's time for them to stop, but that depends on their will power. Can people really stop when they are faced with their dark side? Can they really integrate their own shadow into their normal lives? Since the first baby was born, his shadow was also born. Sun cast that shadow on us like a spell since birth. The closer you get to the sun the bigger your shadow is on the ground. Therefore, there is no point in trying to choose sides. All we can do is choose who we want to be and be it, but whatever you choose – don't choose *normal*. Anything, but *normal*."

He stopped talking. He looked pleased with himself and took a sip of water. This shit was making so much sense. This was the best speech I had ever heard in my life. I started clapping also. I was elated.

Joe was beaming and said, "Thank you gentlemen. Oh yeah, I forgot to ask you, which batch did you like the best?"
Roman said, "Joey, we already forgot why we came here."

We all laughed then Roman looked at me and said, "Oh yeah, give us some of that white widow magic." I nodded.

Joe said, "I will be back, meanwhile the pool is yours. Jump in. I got some important clients coming in twenty minutes, so don't be long." He left inside the house through the glass door.

Roman took his clothes off and jumped in like a bomb. I followed him. Jose stayed sitting, looking at us. We swam in that picturesque pool while I observed our shadows following us on the pool's floor. It was trippy. We got out, dried, put our clothes back on, and Joe returned.

He threw our bag on the table and said, "Here is your prescription guys. It will be fifty bucks. Use it wisely." We gave him our last fifty and thanked him for everything. He shook our hands and said, "Mario will show you guys out. It was my pleasure meeting you. Hopefully, I will meet you again on the road. Good luck to you bozos. Keep crashing their reality." He turned to Jose, shook his hand and said, "Nos veremos de nuevo. Buena suerte viejo amigo." (We will meet again. Good luck old friend.) We shook hands, and Mario the security guard showed us to our car.

We went outside and felt surreal, as if it was all a dream. I got behind the wheel and drove back the same way we came. Llamas were still standing there chewing on grass. As we were getting on the highway I looked in the rear view mirror and saw three big SUVs with tinted windows waiting for the gate to Joe's ranch to open. Usually, government officials used those SUVs. I stepped on the gas, and we drove in silence out of Texas. Roman was writing something. Jose was sleeping on the back seat. We drove all the way into the night, until I was feeling tired and very sleepy. As we entered Arizona, we got off the highway, found the cheapest motel, and got a room. I passed out in my clothes on one bed, Roman on the other, and Jose on the floor with nothing but a blanket to cover himself.

Chapter 12

Arizona Weirdness

I looked at the sign and it read,

"Jesus Fucked Up Again!"

Photoshoot in the Cacti

The next morning, after the hotel provided us with a few continental breakfasts, we were sitting with our cigarettes in our mouths and witnessing the great Western landscape through the windshield. Our Mexican amigo was combing his hair and driving at the same time. We were now passing through Arizona, the land of red rocks and cacti. We started seeing the cacti right by the highway; some of them were small, some were mid-size, but occasionally, we saw really big ones. There was this one tuft of land with cacti and rocks no tourist could resist. Remembering that we were sort of tourists, we stopped to take some pictures next to them.

Now that we had a bag of really good weed, we rolled ourselves a nice sized joint each and smoked them in the car. Roman thought we should dress up and ask people for money next to this really huge cactus. We thought it would look very picturesque and straight out of a western movie, so we went to our car to pick our costumes. Jose looking at us probably thought, "those gringos are weird," and he went for a walk into the cacti forest. The first costume we picked out was a Confederate flag as a skirt, sleeping cushion around my neck and a piece of cardboard box with scribbles on it, *We Need Help*. Roman grabbed a guitar and sat down on the rock playing some Russian songs, or more like yelling them. Of course no one stopped. The people that saw us were speeding away, as soon as they caught a glimpse of a duo of psychos wearing a confederate flags as skirts. We got bored pretty quickly with the begging ceremony so we decided to just have a photo shoot in this random cacti wilderness. We tried on clothes that we found in his SUV to get the right look. Finally, my super duper outfit for this bizarre photo shoot was chosen! I was wearing something that was a cross between a jockey's hamlet and a British policeman hat, open orange shirt, sandals, black punk shorts, from which an American flag was hanging, and of course my broken hand with a cast on it. I was holding a classy umbrella with dark and light blue stripes. Roman looked at me and raised his eyebrow. He had a look on his face of an art director that knew something was missing from this scene. He thought about it for a moment, scratched his head, and went back to the car. He took out a piece of mat, on which you usually sit when it gets cold at night, and wrote on it something with a black marker. When he came back he told me to grab the sign he just made. He said, "With the other hand, you hold onto the umbrella."

I looked at the sign and it read, "Jesus Fucked Up Again!" I started laughing. What a brilliant fucking sign. No more needed to be said. Roman aimed to take the picture. "1,2,3," – he counted down. "Ok please turn your head to the right. Now to the left." – he kept snapping pictures with the cheap plastic camera he had stolen from the local gas station. I looked like I was some kind of a fucked up vaudevillian circus sideshow performer. After taking a few more photos with this large cactus in the background, we returned to the car fully satisfied with ourselves and got back on the highway.

By midday, it was hot and humid. The temperature was exceeding 105 Fahrenheit. In this weather, your brain felt soggy and thirsty for a cold shower and a cold beer. I really wanted to see the Grand Canyon, but we learned there was a major forest fire in the surrounding area. We had no choice but to drive around the Grand Canyon straight to California.

Chapter 13

Roman's Dinosaurs

Jesus, what did I tell you when you got in my car?

My car equals my rules!

Exploring the Dinosaurs inside Roman's Mind

Roman was edgy again. The air around him was heavier than usual, and he didn't want to talk about it. I felt that the closer we were getting to California, the more something was eating him up inside, and it was gnawing on him like a dog on a bone.

"Dimon, can you change that song, I can't hear it anymore!"

I replied, "I like it, it's Auktzion!"

He retorted, "Sounds like bunch of annoying dudki(flutes)! Come on, where is my Eminem?"

I said. "Fuck your hip hop shit!"

He ripped back at me, "Jesus, what did I tell you when you got in my car. My car equals my rules! Where are my cigarettes? What the hell do you do with them all the time? Shit… "

I knew he was just looking for a reason to get at someone, so I tried to stay out of his way.

Chapter 14

California, Final Trials and Triumphs

She leaned forward and the snake's mouth

turned into a woman's lips and

she kissed me long and deep.

Welcome to California

As we all know, the last step is always the hardest. To get to Los Angeles, we had to drive through the Mojave Desert. I had never been to the desert before, and I didn't know what it looked like. I'd read about it, and seen it in the movies, but this time we had to drive through it. We got a tip from an older couple at the gas station to pass through the desert either at dusk or in the morning. We asked if there was a reason why. The older man looked at us for a moment and said, "In the afternoon, the road gets so hot your tires can blow, and trust me you don't want to be waiting for the tow truck in this heat. At night, in the desert your thoughts turn into reality so be careful what you are thinking of," and they quickly drove away. I thought to myself that was a strange thing to say.

Hypnosis

We were entering the Mojave Desert, and we felt things changing. The sand surrounded us, and the road was the only reminder of civilization. The sun was setting to the right. There were single houses here and there, but heat was unbearable, even for a coyote. Roman was driving. Jose was sleeping in the back. I was in the passenger's seat pulling on a fresh joint. We were silent. We drove at dusk, as the old guy recommended.

In most jailbreak movies the prisoners escaped through the desert and you saw nothing for miles, only the melting asphalt as the car zoomed past the camera. We were in a similar scenario. Sand dunes all around us made a perfect backdrop for a movie set. Time was standing still, and you were left alone to your own thoughts. Roman's eyes were transfixed on the road. It seemed as if we were entering a different country, and we had to be very careful not to disobey the rules, not to anger the only true resident of this desolate place: the sun. The desert was the sun's playground, and it could be a ruthless predator if you didn't obey its rules.

I was in the passenger seat staring directly at the car lights in front of me, and I was under its motionless spell. My eyes were half-closed. The two red lights of the car in front of me slowly turned into the eyes of the snake, and I remembered from an occult book I read somewhere: "When you see a snake, that means you are going to the next level of consciousness." It looked like a cobra with two ruby eyes. I saw her arise from the white line of the road, her head raised above the hood of the car looking back at me, staring directly into my eyes. Her eyes were hypnotizing me, and I slid into some parallel reality. My head fell on my shoulder. I closed my eyes for a moment. I saw in the distance a lonely man descending from a sand dune. He looked like a Native American walking with his head down. His clothes were made of yellow leather, ripped in a few places with patches of blood here and there. He looked like he was coming from some battle. He was following a snake, which was winding and unwinding in front of him showing him the way. The snake's eyes were crystals that she used to illuminate the way.

A short distance away, a coyote was following them. The coyote would run for a while then sit on the sand, whimpering a little, and then continue the pursuit. The coyote knew in the desert the old king, the Sun, burned away all the water, and if the Native American didn't find his way out, the coyote would get to polish his bones. All of a sudden his guide, the desert snake, stopped and slithered back to his feet. The Native American stopped and was staring at her, not sure what to do next. Winding and unwinding in rings, the snake started crawling up his leg. At first he was taken aback, but then he realized that it's there to show him the way out, so he surrendered. The snake climbed to his shoulders and whispered into his ear, "There are powers that show us the Great Spirit that dwells within us all. You are a lost soul, and you have lost the connection to your body. I am going show you a way back." She made her way back down to the ground and started winding and unwinding towards the car. The Native American followed her.

By now I felt like we had stopped moving. The closer she got to the car, the more frightened I became. When this procession got close, I could finally see the Native American's eyes were hollow and black inside. As the snake climbed up through my half opened window and onto my lap, she made one circle around my neck and looked me straight in the eyes. I was yelling, but no sound came out of my mouth. She leaned forward, and the snake's mouth turned into a woman's lips. She kissed me long and deep. It was the most seductive and most passionate kiss I have ever felt in my life. Instead of the snake's tongue, it was a woman's tongue. I stopped screaming.

Soul Retrieval

I felt the Native American grab me by my shoulders as he started shaking me. He was mumbling something, I couldn't tell what he was saying, but I could make out the words, "I am your spirit, and I've come back to your body! I am your spirit, and I've come back to your body!"

While he was shaking me, I realized he was my soul. My soul was the Native American who was lost in the desert, and it is I who came to collect it. I was shaking. At that last thought, the Native American took one step towards me, and then he jumped right inside my body. I got a jolt of intense energy rushing to my head. I was transported to a different place. I saw the pattern of how I lost my soul.

My love betrayed me. I started seeing scenes where my lovers were leaving me, or saying something that hurt me deep inside. Eventually, without trying to reason or a way out, I just closed my heart to all the hurt. I put it into a protected cell where nothing could reach me. I was dead to the things that I loved, and what was left was my brain; my mind. In my dream, I remembered a woman with tarot cards in front of me, telling me my soul is not with me. It's wandering in the desert. I have to go and get it. I became soulless and numb and ran from every opportunity where I could find a way out of this imprisonment. I was too afraid. Now I felt like screaming. I opened my mouth, and black ants were escaping from my mouth. Hundreds, thousands, millions were rushing away from my body.

"Ahhhhhhhhhhhhhhhhhhh," I was yelling.

I felt someone shaking me, trying to wake me up. I was coming to my senses. I could hear Roman's voice, "Dimon, what's the matter with you? Wake Up! Why are you screaming?"

He was shaking me. "Are you ok?"

I opened my eyes, and said, "What are you doing? Where am I? What was that?"

Roman said, "You were having a bad dream. You drive now. I am falling asleep."

I couldn't believe I was just having a dream. Everything seemed so real. I sat there, staring at the dark in front of me. As I was coming to my senses and stepping out of the car, I saw another vision, only this time it came from the sky. As I stood up, the stars above me started shooting left and right over the mountains in the background all at the same time, and I was witnessing the greatest vision. The whole sky was filled with streaks of star tails in the dark night sky, and the stars kept shooting and shooting left and right, a rain of stardust. They were falling as if all secret wishes that people made were coming true right at that moment, and I was witnessing it. It was magnificent. I was shivering from the realization and acceptance of what I was seeing with my eyes.

I looked back at the car to see where Roman and Jose were, but they were asleep. I was standing there and the world stopped and I was the only one who saw it and I was thankful to the road that brought me to this place. This was the most magical moment of the whole road trip. I yelled at the dark sky, "Thank you. I will take it with me until I die!" After that I closed my eyes and felt a great rush of energy flood my whole body.

Pass the Peace Pipe

Finally, I got into the car. I started driving and singing out loud, "Eha waha, eha wahahey pass that pipe, Lone Wolf." Lone Wolf passed me a long wooden pipe with smoke coming out of the other end. I inhaled and sang, "Eha waha, ehooooo - The Great Spirit gave me a good sign today."

The Lone Wolf said, "Ahhh, you and your signs Half Horse, we have been going hungry for a long time now, and we haven't spotted any deer, where are your signs when we need them?" Lone Wolf was hungry and irritated.

"Eha waha wahaaa ooo," - I continued, "Hey right there, there is one. Look!"

The Lone Wolf looked and said, "Half Horse, You smoke too much of that pipe, it's a tree!"

I retorted, "No you smoke too much, Lone Wolf, otherwise you would go and get my bow and arrow."

Lone Wolf squinted and exclaimed, "Ohhh Great Kaka! It's a deer! You are right, Half Horse! We got us a nice meal tonight."

I continued singing, "Eha waha, waha waha. Eha, waha waha waha. Hey Lone Wolf, but who needs a meal when we have a nice pipe, pass that pipe, let that deer live."

Lone Wolf thought about it for a moment and said, "Yeah Half Horse you are right. Why kill a nice looking deer?" - and they both took turns inhaling clear blue smoke into their lungs and forgot all about the deer and the fact that they were hungry. They got really stoned and stared at the coyote that was crossing the road.

I couldn't drive anymore it was dusk. I took the first exit, found a place to park and turned off the headlights. We all fell asleep right in the car since no one could drive anymore.

Final Destination LA, California

We were on the last leg of our road trip. We were 100 miles away from LA, and we made it in about 2 hours. The city was covered by dusk. The city we were slowly and persistently driving to resembled a giant beast with arms whose veins were rows of lights and illuminated houses.

Jose asked us to let him out. We agreed it was a good time to let him go. We let Jose out at the parking lot of the convenience store. Just like that, he left the same way he came. He just said, "Thank You Amigos."

We shook hands. I felt bad for him, so I reached into my jeans and found 10 dollars. I gave it to him and added, "Wish I had more."

He said, "Gracias. Thank You."

I wasn't sure how far that would take him, but at least he could buy himself his next meal. He just walked out into the night, probably to look for a place to stay, or for another ride to take him further inland. We knew we were never going to see this odd little guy again so we kept staring at him as he was walking away. He took out his hair brush and combed his hair as a sign of reassurance. For that one moment, I wanted to believe that we somehow changed his life and sent him on a good path, and that thought was a comforting one.

That same evening we arrived at Roman's parent's house.

Chapter 15

LA or The Royal Court

His mom looked up from her plate with a worried face,
"What do you mean, hang your flags? Where you get those flags?
My flowers grow there!"

Roman's Headquarters

His parent's house looked like a regular middle class family house. There was nothing special about it from the outside. His parents were actually very nice and welcoming people, as you'd expect from any traditional Eastern European family. Upon our arrival, his mom started running around and repeating how hungry we must be and that she was preparing food for us immediately. His father was a somber, heavyset man, with a bald spot, grey hair and a very classic Russian look about him: white tank encompassing his large stomach, sporty Adidas pants and flip-flops. He just said, "Ahh, nu nakonetz to. Nadoelo shlyatsya?" (Ahh, finally. Had enough of vagabounding?) Dinner was being served and we were called to the table shortly.

From the moment we sat down to eat, it was their time to ask Roman an endless series of annoying questions: what is he going to do with the expiring car lease, with his job, with himself? How does he expect to pay for all the credit card bills piling up? He looked bored. "No wonder", I thought, my parents were similar, and I wouldn't want to be answering all those questions the minute I walked into the house. No wonder the guy traveled all the time.

His father relentlessly kept on, announcing Roman's ex-wife has been interested in finding out where he's been. At that question he just kind of chuckled, "Yeah, why?" He didn't want to find out, so he turned to me and said, "Dimon, we have to hang our flags in the backyard to celebrate our arrival. Let's make it look like a medieval court. It will be magnificent!"

His mom looked up from her plate with a worried face, "What do you mean, hang your flags? Where you get those flags? My flowers grow there!"

He yelled as he was running towards the garage, "Mamon, don't worry it will look splendid."

After the third week of putting our ideas into reality, we quickly went about gathering tools and a ladder to hang our flags. In about 10 minutes we hung one British, one Australian, and one Canadian in his family's backyard. We attached the flags hanging down from the ceiling, sticking the flagpoles in the tall sidewall with grapevines growing on it. They made the whole backyard look like the medieval court of some noble king. After that, we walked by the flags and gave each other a noble greeting by saying, "Welcome noble Sir to Royal Court." His parents apparently were used to Roman's jokes and pranks, they just stood there and stared with disapproval, hoping his ideas didn't involve changing the shape of their garden, trees, backyard, or the whole house.

Banya & Vobla

After that, he turned to me and pronounced, "Dimon, let's go to *Banya* and have some beer with vobla." (*Banya* – a Russian sauna made of wood to keep the heat inside. *Vobla* – dried fish that is best to be eaten with beer - great tasting with a seriously strong smell.) That sounded pretty awesome, since I haven't been to the *Banya* in a very long time, and his father had one built right in his backyard. Going to *Banya* was a Russian tradition that I grew up with, where all the men of the family would go and sit there for hours discussing global affairs. Everyone wore a wool hat over their ears and every 20 minutes they would splash ice-cold water on each other, and repeat the procedure until they turned into red lobsters. After that, being all sweaty, they would gather with their towels around their waist, and they would drink beer and eat lots of smelly, great tasting vobla. Then they would either continue with vodka shots, or chase it all with tea and Prianiki (big vanilla cookies). Yep, that's the tradition, and if you go around any Russians and ask them if they like to go to *Banya*, they would smile and proudly say yes, because every Russian loves *Banya*.

We ran to *Banya* with our towels, and his father was already sitting there all red and sweaty. He was saying, "Davai davai, zakhodi (Come on, enter.) Close the door quickly, don't let heat out, I throw some wood in the fire." His father seemed more relaxed and happier now that his son was home. Although it was in a very Russian, tough love kind of way. His look was saying, I am happy to see you, but don't get too happy. You got things to do. His father wore a wool hat over his eyes and asked slyly, "Any interesting women stories?"

We looked at each other and started laughing. Roman said, "Papanya, you don't want to know, but let's just say we had fun."

Father said, "Ok as long as you wore the gloves I told you." He chuckled and continued, "I don't want grandchildren all over United States."

Roman said, "No grand children don't worry, but I did meet one special girl. I will tell you about her later."

Father answered, "Tell me when you are serious about someone. I have had enough of your flip-flop attitude," and he made a flip flop sound with his flip-flops. We laughed and his father smiled at his own joke. His father reminded me of my own dad. Many Russian fathers spoke in a similar way.

We were sweating in Roman's father's sauna. It was almost surreal – we were finally here. We could relax and kick back. It felt familiar now, sitting in this sweaty room. We had come to a final stop, and that feeling of satisfaction of having completed our journey started to grow inside of me. There were no more questions of how to get gas, where we are going to eat, and where we are going to sleep. We did it all. We were just sitting in the sauna sweating, and when it was too hot to stay inside, we ran outside, opened our beers, and started drinking in gulps.

His mom brought us some pierogies with meat and cabbage, and we started hungrily eating like we hadn't eaten in those three weeks. Everything was available. There was enough food for us to stuff ourselves until we couldn't move, and that's exactly what we did. We stuffed ourselves like turkeys on Thanksgiving, and when we finished, we polished it with beers and some tea. That day was amazing! Roman went inside. I stayed outside, swinging on the hammock with my feet down while the flags swayed over my head, as if it was some kind of a trophy. I had my ticket booked to leave LA in the next two days, so for two days I was going hang out around LA. That same night, his parents arranged for me to sleep in a nice bed, and that was my first night sleeping comfortably without a worry in the world. The moment my head touched the pillow, I slipped into a dreamless sleep.

Roman's Truth Uncovered

Next morning we had a full breakfast, and Roman's parents arranged for him to meet up with his ex-wife. When we walked outside to smoke a cigarette, I said to him, "You don't seem too happy about seeing your ex-wife."

He fell silent. In a few moments he replied, "I gotta go and see my kid man."

He reached out for his wallet and this time I saw him taking out a few photographs from inside, and it hit me that those were the same photographs he was probably showing to John from the trailer park in Florida. I remembered how they were bonding on the family and kids, and I didn't even care to take a look at the photographs. I was too busy judging them. He handed me two photographs. On one, there was a couple: a very happy, well-groomed Roman dressed in a black suit, hugging a girl with dark brown hair, pretty in a very natural kind of way. I looked at the second photo, and there was a little baby girl on it, about 2 years old, with a blue hat, grinning at the camera. I said, "So you are a father then!" Roman sighed heavily, "Not a good one I guess." I asked the question I have been meaning to ask him the whole trip, "So is that why you drive back and forth?"

He looked lost as he was pulling on his mustache. He took a long drag from his cigarette and said, "We were high school sweethearts, and then we got married and had a kid. We named her Julia. One night, my wife told me we have to buy a house. I didn't want to buy a house. I didn't want to take out this huge loan that I will work for the rest of my life for. She insisted, so we started checking out some houses for sale. She said we either move into the house, or we split up. I didn't know what to do, so I waited. I wasn't going to jump into a 30-year loan and be in debt my whole life just because she wanted it. It hit me that this is what my life will be for the rest of my days: Wife, kid, work, and my crazy parents. I couldn't take it man! It was driving me nuts. I thought if I live like this, I was going to get a disease, like cancer or something. That's how it starts, you know, from wrong choices you make, and that will be the end of me and then one day, I saw her with my best friend. I knew this kid since high school and he betrayed me. It looked like they were getting comfortable with each other. They kissed while they were holding hands. My wife was cheating on me with my best friend. I guess she couldn't wait for me anymore. He was definitely the settling down type. I didn't want to ask questions. I just took off. I got in the car and drove." He was silent. Hurt, and still in love.

I understood. If I were in the same situation right now, I would freak out too. I just said, "Come on man. It's ok. It's your life right? You make your choices and you live it how you want it," - at least that's what you told me. There was silence - he was smoking.

He was hurt, and I could see his real emotions coming without any laughter or tricks attached to them. He was regretting and fighting his own feelings. He was conflicted. I understood what was eating him inside and what drove him to cross the USA over and over again.

A few years later, after many breakups with my fiancé, I was laying unconscious on the streets of New York too drunk to remember how I ended up there. I was robbed one of those times. Next time, I broke my jaw falling down the stairs drunk. I would sleep with women just to cover a void, but the void only grew wider and deeper. A broken heart is hard to repair, but only time heals all wounds. Finally, I went skydiving. When I was falling, I thought I was going to die. When I landed on the ground safely, I realized I would be ok from then on. My life started all over again.

The stories are endless, but the outcome is the same. We get over the failed promises and go on living with a much stronger heart and with greater wisdom. Another thing that seemed really immature to me was how I didn't see that the person next to me was going through this whole break up and torment. I was too busy worrying about fitting everything in my head into the appropriate shelves.

Venice Beach, LA

We parted ways, and he left me the car to get around Los Angeles if I wanted to. The first thing I wanted to do was to drive up to Venice Beach where my favorite band, *The Doors,* got their start. Also, I really wanted to check out the scene at the famous Sunset Strip Boulevard. I took his stick shift operated Jeep that we crossed the country in and, after few jerks and the smell of burnt clutch, I finally pulled out of the parking spot. I still sucked at driving with a stick shift.

There was only a brief period of time, when I drove a stick shift. I was seventeen, and I was working as a valet parking attendant at a middle eastern restaurant. My friend and I would take really expensive cars for a ride around the parking lot to learn how to drive a stick. After one car finally died on me, and I had to tell the owner, I decided the stick shift was not for me. Luckily, the owner was plastered out of his mind and the belly dancer's hips were still dancing in his eyes, so he didn't really care about his car immobile in the parking lot.

I hoped the same fate didn't happen to me and Roman's car. I finally arrived at Venice Beach, parked the car, and started walking towards the beach. It was a breezy afternoon. The sun was shining on the few people that were there at that hour, since it was a Wednesday afternoon. People were at work. I sat down in the sand and smoked the rest of the last joint. I wondered if people saw how Jim Morrison and Ray Manzarek hung out at this beach. Ray asked Jim to read him a poem, and with that they opened the doors of their own perception. What a time that must have been. I don't think it looked any different than today. The air of possibility and chance was blowing. I pondered on all those thoughts for a while and then turned back to walk to the car.

After that, I drove through the Sunset Strip. I realized what a tacky place it had become. I am sure that without all the coffee shops, stores and sport bars, it was a more vivid place at night, but the sun was just setting. It felt like the normal people were out to hunt you, so I quickly left the scene.

Times they are a-changin'! I am sure that somewhere else, maybe on the other side of the globe a new underground city or society might be flourishing. The old Babylon might be fading, but the new Babylon is always rising through the cracks in the ground to flourish once again. It's like an earthworm. You never know where it will spring up next.

I got a cup of coffee and headed back to Roman's house, since I was to board a plane back to NYC the next morning. I needed to pack. On the way back, I got lost. Jerking the car back and forth, sweating bullets, I eventually arrived back at his house, swearing to God never to operate a stick shift again.

The Last Evening

Back at his house, I found Roman in the best mood ever. I had never seen him like that. He told me that he had visited his ex-wife and saw his daughter and that it was the best thing he did this summer. He reported that his little girl was growing, and she already knew how to tie her own shoelaces. "Wow! What a change in Roman," I thought to myself. He looked truly happy. I thought that would never happen. I told him I was very happy for him, too. After I asked him how his ex was, I wished I hadn't. He just looked away and said, "The same, still wanting a house."

Not wanting to go on with the conversation, I told him, "All right, I got to go and pack."

The same evening, an old friend of my family was supposed to come for a dinner. He was a poet and a professional masseur at the same time. His name was Seoma. He was an odd man, always smiling. I knew him since childhood and was looking forward to seeing him. When he came around, we greeted each other, immediately had six cups of tea, some snacks, cheese, and sandwiches, a big tea party feast. I told him about our trip, and then I noticed Roman's parents were really enjoying talking to him. Roman and I trailed off to the side, allowing them to enjoy each other's company.

At Roman's royal court we finished our last joint. Our flags, the trophies from the road, were swaying over our heads. In the corner of my eye, I noticed Seoma standing and reading his poetry out loud to Roman's parents, which I thought was pretty amazing. The poet and his audience found each other. I could have sworn that I saw Roman's father shed a tear. Up to this day, I think Seoma still visits their house to read some poetry. Russians love poetry.

The last evening passed quietly. We were just sipping on some tea. Roman's parents spoke to me briefly, wished me a good trip back home, and since they didn't know me, they thanked me for arriving home with their son whom they haven't seen for a while, and for their newly founded friend. After that everyone went to sleep.

Roman and I were just sitting there, munching on some cookies, kind of just kicking around the topic of me going back to living with Vlad. It was not a very exciting prospect for me at that time, but it was my home nevertheless.

After a while, I said, "Yeah man, I don't think I could have gone on a cross country trip all by myself because all my friends are too scared and too busy to take a trip like that."

Roman said, "Yeah, it was quite a trip, I think it was the best cross country trip I ever had, or ever will! Ha!" Then he took off in an instant and yelled back at me, "Dimon, I got a present for you!

He came back with the biggest grin on his face and handed me a large piece of cloth. When I opened it, I realized it was huge, brown colored lady's underwear. I am talking about fat lady's underwear. We started laughing really loud. That was some gift. I put it over my head, and we laughed even louder.

He exclaimed, "Oh wait! I have to autograph it." He grabbed a pen and wrote on the ass area, in Russian, "Gruzite apelsini iazshikami!" – *Ostap Bender*. The translation meant, "Load the oranges by boxes!"

Ostap Bender is the quintessential Soviet (and at the same time, anti-Soviet) character. The anti-hero in one of the most beloved Russian novels of all time, Ilf and Petrov's "The Twelve Chairs."

That was the most perfect gift. I didn't expect to receive any other type of a gift from Roman. On that note we ended the last day of our road trip. I went to sleep so I would be well rested for my trip back to NYC.

Chapter 16

The Return

If tomorrow the planet will turn over and stop carrying us forward, I will be able to say that I lived, I laughed and I cried, and I didn't deny myself a chance to be on the road.

Flying Back over the Road

I was sitting in my airplane seat with a bag full of washed clothes, and my cast around my arm. I was thinking of going back to living with Vlad, and the debt I owed my mother for this trip, but somehow I knew something would turn up, and I would take care of those things because an experience like this is priceless. You can't teach it. Three hours into the flight, the voice on the intercom announced we were at the altitude of thirteen thousand feet above the ground. I looked down from the futuristic airplane window; the sun was blazing, and there were little squares of the crop fields and highways spread out like huge snakes across the land. A tiny speck of a car was moving on the highway. About a week ago, I could have been in that car on my road trip.

I thought about everything that happened: all the accidents, incidents, laughs, kicks, illegal activities, two broken bones in my left arm, and it seemed like it couldn't have happened in two and a half weeks. It felt as if I was cleansed of all that I'd known two and a half weeks before. I felt as if the wind from the road settled in my body forever. I was free and ready for anything, because nothing seemed impossible. I have seen, felt and experienced the life on the road, and I lost my identity. I was Russian and not Russian. I was American and not American. I belonged to the road.

Flying over the land that we'd crossed made me realize that this is the way I chose to experience freedom. Other people choose it by taking hallucinogenic drugs, or by drinking, or other extremes without going anywhere, but I chose this way. I could have easily taken a plane to LA, hung out there, spent money on hotels and other bullshit local attractions, but instead I chose to see every mile along the way.

Those are the innocent and spontaneous times of our lives we call youth. What we are and what we become is a combination of all those times when we said YES to freedom from the everyday routine, and we accepted the unknown as our only guide. That feeling carried us forward into the new dimension of experiencing life on this planet we call Earth. Once you let go of all material possessions and needs and wants, it really is the simplest experiences that end up being the most memorable ones. We love life when we make a choice. If tomorrow the planet turns over and stops carrying us forward, I will be able to say that I lived. I smoked my joints, I laughed, I cried, and I didn't deny myself a chance to be on the road. The most prophetic sages and yogis of India try to achieve the most basic state of existence, which is to see the world as if you had never seen it before.

If you should start pondering on whether you should take a road trip, I would say YES! Because any road you choose is the same road. All roads lead to the same place, but everyone's way of getting there is different. The passengers and drivers that help us get there may change, but the most profound feeling we can share as people is traveling together.

If my story will help you to start on your own adventure, then let it happen to you, because someone helped me find my road and now, you owe it to yourself to find the road that sets you free.

I closed my eyes and I was on the road again, only now I also had big brown ladies' underwear in my suitcase.

- Dmitry Wild

Roman and his new friend

Roman and John inspecting the insides of a Green Dinosaur

Why be Normal?

The Road

Meanwhile in New Mexico

Cowboys and Indians

Jesus Fucked Up Again

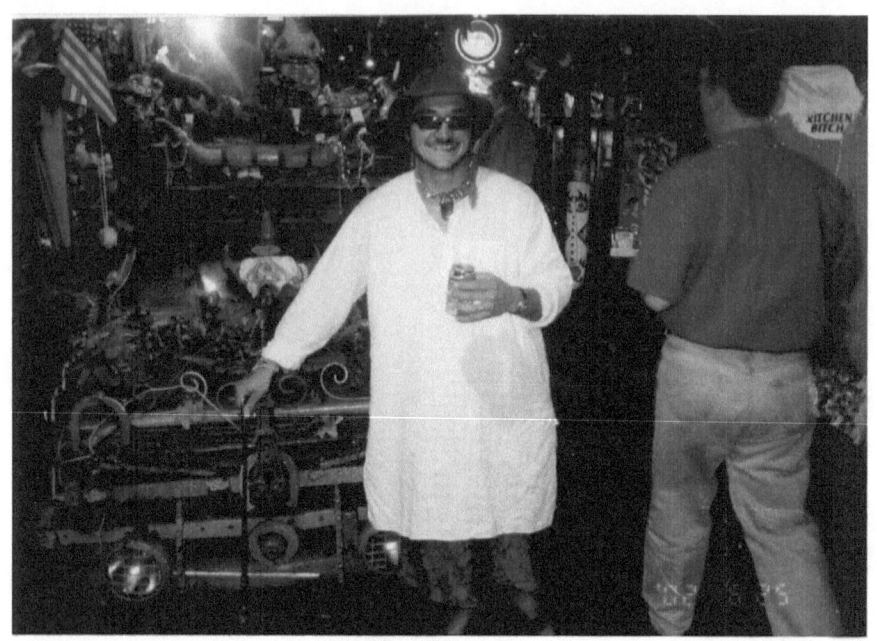

New Orleans

New Orleans

We need help or Photoshoot in the desert

At King's Court

www.ingramcontent.com/pod-product-compliance
Lightning Source LLC
Chambersburg PA
CBHW050029180626
46810CB00002B/646